Macushla
and other stories...

YVONNE T. TIBBS

*To Mark & Josie
with love,
Yvonne Tibbs*

© Yvonne T. Tibbs 2018

Print ISBN: 978-1-54395-483-8

eBook ISBN: 978-1-54395-484-5

All rights reserved. This book or any portion thereof may not be reproduced or used in any manner whatsoever without the express written permission of the publisher except for the use of brief quotations in a book review.

I would like to dedicate this book to all the people who have helped me with their support and input with a special nod to my husband, Mark, and my number one fan, Ms. Kay Roach

CHAPTER 1

Peg tossed her empty Red Bull can into the weeds alongside the road. *Since when are you a litterbug?* Leaving the window down, she leaned back to let the crisp evening air revive her senses. To the west, cornstalks were ablaze with crimson and gold, but Peg kept her eyes on the road. Sunsets always reminded her of Jake.

Lately, everything reminded her of Jake.

Tonight will be different. Tonight, I'm gonna have some fun!

Four years of nursing school by day and waitressing at night had been rough. But, man was it worth it! Because of that degree, Peg was finally able to high-tail it out of her hometown of Divinity, (nothing divine about it) Kentucky and leave her lying-ass, cheating boyfriend behind.

Good nurses were needed everywhere.

"The destination is on your right," the GPS stated.

Peg looked to see a string of cars parked bumper to bumper on a long cobblestone driveway. After nudging her secondhand Ford in behind a late model Bentley, she leaned out the window for a peek. Unlike the hills and gullies back home, northern Ohio was flat allowing her a clear view of her hostess's hacienda-style home. Peg stared at it open-mouthed.

Sprawled across what looked like a quarter of an acre, the two-story home with its many windows, alcoves, and balconies was nothing short of breathtaking. Was this the right place? She pulled out her iPhone. Yep, this was it.

Despite her aversion to sunsets, as the waning daylight bathed the home in a saffron-tinted haze, Peg found that she couldn't look away. After the sun retreated, leaving only artificial light to defray the gloom, the home took on a more sinister aura. Hands trembling, she freshened her lipstick.

"You look fine," she told the rearview mirror. "Now get your ass inside."

Peg climbed out of the car, looked down, and swore under her breath. The hem of her little black skirt was creeping up her thighs again. All those nights alone with Netflix and take-out were beginning to show. Yanking it back in place, she strode up the driveway, heels clacking against the cobbles, heart thudding inside her chest.

She'd thought making friends would be easy. So far, however, there was only Fred, the one-eyed tabby cat she found in a dumpster. But, things were about to change. A flashy blonde who worked alongside Peg at the hospital, Sasha, hadn't seemed very friendly before. In fact, her "out of the blue" invitation to her boyfriend's birthday bash took Peg by surprise. Still, a party was a party, and that's just what she needed.

As she neared the house, a wave of party music gushed out to greet her. Fast and funky, it lured her past the dark mahogany doors in front and into a long latticed tunnel affixed to one side of the house.

When she emerged, the cobbles fanned out beneath her feet as a star-studded sky reeled overhead. The scent of fresh air and grilling meat was tantalizing and the music, louder now, seemed to pulsate through her veins. Blinking, Peg scanned the immense courtyard.

She'd attended lots of parties back home, but never had there been so many people! To her left, a row of two-story high archways lined the back of the house. She slipped behind the nearest one and peeked out at the other guests. Scattered about in loosely formed clusters, the women flaunted cocktail dresses while the men sported button up shirts and blazers.

Just when she'd gathered her courage and was about to join in, Peg felt her muscles clench as an inexplicable feeling of dread washed over her. Something was wrong. *What's the matter with you? Did you come all this way just to chicken out?* She took a deep breath, smoothed her skirt, and dove into the throng.

Minutes later, she spotted her hostess's platinum locks at the center of one of the clusters.

"Peg!" Breaking free, Sasha rushed to her side as if they were long lost friends.

Peg stiffened then tried to relax as the woman embraced her. "This place is amazing!" she heard herself say. "Now, I see why you don't mind the long commute."

Sasha grinned, her snow-white teeth contrasting nicely with her tan. "We kinda like it."

"We?"

"You know, Brad and me."

Peg didn't know.

"Most people call him Dr. Carlson."

Peg was taken aback. The only Dr. Brad Carlson she knew of was head of genetics at the local university. *He* was Sasha's boyfriend? No wonder the house was so grand! She tried to hide the look of shock from her face.

3

Sasha laughed. "Yeah, that's the one. So, how was the drive?"

"Not bad," Peg lied. After working all day, the hour-long journey with nothing to see but cornfields and sky had been mind- numbing.

"Great!" Sasha said, shoving an ice-cold glass into Peg's hand. "Here, you gotta try this."

"I shouldn't." Peg eyed the lime green beverage. "I'll have to drive home later."

Sasha leaned in, her breath warm and ripe with alcohol. "Don't worry, hon. It'll wear off before you leave. And, if it doesn't…" She spread her arms wide. "We have lots of guest rooms."

Peg envisioned a candlelit chamber with king-size bed, private bath, and a balcony overlooking the courtyard. Placing the glass to her lips, she tilted her head back and let the fruity concoction glide down her throat.

"Atta girl!" Sasha laughed. "Come on. I'll introduce you around."

Allowing her new friend to lead her by the arm, Peg smiled until her jaws ached. The guests were an eclectic bunch, men and woman of various backgrounds ranging from late teens to a few who were obviously well into their senior years. All appeared glassy-eyed and unsteady.

But then, so am I. Peg glanced at her watch. It was only 10:32, and she'd already lost track of how many drinks she had consumed. Maybe driving to a late night party after working a twelve-hour shift wasn't such a good idea after all. Now, the ground felt like rubber and the muscles in her legs were starting to twitch. Spotting some tables and chairs by a large swimming pool at the back of the yard, she excused herself.

Peg lowered herself into a lounge chair and leaned back to gaze at the lights reflected atop the water. Almost at once, her limbs fell lax and her eyelids drooped. *Stop it! How would it look if you got caught snoring?*

As she adjusted her chair to the upright position, Peg noticed something on the table beside her. Funny. Why hadn't she seen it before? She reached out and touched a small book with a cool, smooth cover. Picking it up, she was surprised by how light it felt in her hands.

Peg turned it this way and that but found no markings whatsoever. When she opened it, the paper had a strange almost sticky quality and… That was weird. There was text on the first ten pages or so, but the rest were blank. She flipped back to the title page, which read "The Unexplored" with no reference to the copyright, publisher, or even who wrote it. Peg turned to the beginning, eyes skimming over the prose. Moments later, she was ensconced in the tale.

Yvonne T. Tibbs

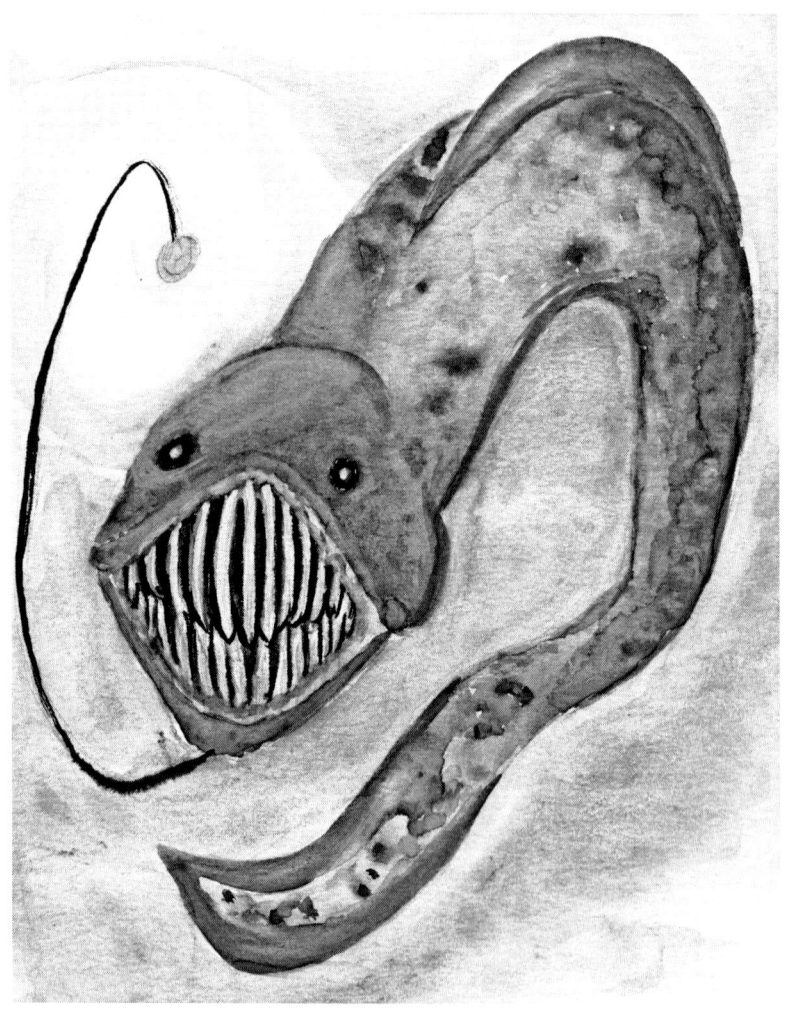

CHAPTER 2
The Unexplored

My colleagues warned me of how it would be - the darkness, the tedium, the agonizingly cramped quarters. But, they didn't know, *couldn't* have known, the worst of it.

I cannot bear to look out that porthole again. Those newly discovered bottom-feeders my associates refer to as phantom fish are probably still there… watching me. If not them, something far worse.

I'm aware that what I'm saying is implausible. Living in these lightless depths, those ethereal fish with their translucent bodies and winglike fins are, most certainly, blind. They're probably just attracted to certain vibrations given off by this craft. Yet, I would've sworn those membrane-covered organs were following my every move.

It's hard not to believe one's own senses.

The objective was to spend two weeks in this, the deepest part of the earth ever reached by humankind, collecting as much data as possible. We've already learned much of this oceanic trench with the aid of remotely operated vehicles. Imagine our surprise when we found an entire sea running beneath it.

It was on the fifth day, I first noticed the unsettling phenomena. Those pallid fish that had been gliding by my portholes for days suddenly converged on my craft and appeared to be peering in at me. Later on, something even more disturbing yet, at that time, thrilling occurred.

Night and and day look exactly the same here in the deep, and even though the computer logs everything, I pride myself on keeping abreast of the time. After seeing *him*, however, I seem to have lost the ability. According to my records, it was on the seventh day that I detected a flurry of movement outside the porthole. I looked up to see the phantom fish scatter as a dark, man-sized being approached my craft. Jet-black with a barb-encrusted tail, the animal's elongated body glistened like diamonds in a lakebed. Its head was enormous with icicle-like fangs protruding like narrow but deadly swords from its massive jaws. Yet, what struck me most were the creature's eyes. Like giant vats of the blackest ink, I could actually see myself reflected inside them.

Although some might regard this as an impetus for nightmares, my heart leapt with excitement. Hands shaking, I double-checked the equipment. Everything seemed to be operating properly, so I logged the time (21:00 exactly) and signaled to my colleagues above.

"Are you seeing what I'm seeing?"

"What?" a sleepy voice responded.

It was O'Conner. Peering into the monitor, his hair was flat on one side, and he was rubbing his eyes. Asleep on the job – *again*.

"Where's Higashi?" I demanded.

"In bed, of course. It's past midnight."

"What? What are you talking about? It's only…" My eyes flicked to the clock in the upper lefthand corner, which read 00:11. Staring at the numbers in disbelief, I reached over to pick up my watch. O'Conner was right. So, what the hell happened to the last three hours?

"Well, wake her ass up!" I shouted.

"Okay, Doc," O'Conner said. "Don't get your panties in a knot."

O'Conner is an idiot.

While waiting, I examined the creature more closely. Another exceptional aspect was the green-tinted glow that radiated from its body. Although bioluminescence occurs widely in deep-sea life, the strange light emitted by this creature was so powerful, it seemed to dispel the outer lights of my craft.

I caught a glimpse of what appeared to be tiny appendages beneath the animal's foremost regions before my attention was wrenched back to its eyes. Unable to look away, as I gazed into those large ebony orbs, I could *feel* the creature seeing me – knowing me, as if it was learning the whole of my existence with merely a look.

As I continued to stare helplessly, a thin incurvate shaft protruding from its chin grew bright with a light of its own. It quivered for a moment then began to sway back and forth. Terror gripped me as the hypnotic motion seemed to pull my body forth while my vessel dissolved around me, and I was sucked ever downward through subterranean passageways, plummeting toward the very core of the earth.

"Dr. Whitman?"

Static crackled in my ear then, with a flip of its tail, my pelagic visitor was gone. Gasping for air, I clutched the arms of my chair to keep from sliding to the floor.

"Dr. Whitman?" A female voice repeated.

I looked to the monitor and saw Higashi, her pretty forehead creased with worry. Nodding my head, I tried to respond but lacked the breath.

"John! What the hell is going on down there?"

"D… Did you see it?" I sputtered.

"What?"

"Camera one, just now."

"No. Something's wrong with the screen. Wait! It's back now."

"You didn't see it?" I clenched the chair's arms tighter.

"Sorry. Must've been some kind of glitch. I was sleeping pretty good, you know." There was an edge to her voice.

"O'Conner still there?" I asked.

"Yeah, Doc," he said. "I'm here."

I leaned back and took a breath. "Tell Higashi what you saw."

"But, I didn't – "

"Are you kidding me?"

"Sorry, Doc. I – "

"Higashi," I said, talking over him. "I think we've discovered an amazing new species. In fact, I'm certain of it."

"Really?" She was wide-awake now.

"Hold on," I said, rewinding the tape, "I'll show you."

As I awaited the awed exclamations of my colleagues, I kept my eyes on the window. Would the creature return? After what just happened, did I really want it to? *Of course, you do*, I chided myself. *This graphene-encased hull is impenetrable. That fearsome brute, whatever it is, can't possibly harm you.*

"I can't see anything," Higashi said.

I looked to see a pale but powerful light suffusing the entire screen. "Shit!" I exclaimed, slamming my fist against the console.

"The camera's fucked up." O'Conner sounded smug. "That's why I couldn't see it."

I wanted to wring his scrawny neck. "There's nothing wrong with the camera," I said. "The creature was emanating some powerful type of phosphorescent light. I'll have to make some adjustments. I'm sorry Higashi, but I'm sure he'll be back."

"How do you know it's a he?" O'Conner asked.

That was actually a good question. There was no way I could've known. Yet somehow, I did.

"In the meantime," I said, addressing Higashi, "why don't you go back to bed."

"What? No! I want to see it."

I admired her enthusiasm, but I myself was having trouble keeping my eyes open. "And, you will. I just think we should rest up in the meantime. I promise, if he shows so much as a toenail, I'll send O'Conner to get you."

"Yeah," O'Conner said. "Go on. I'll make sure you don't miss anything."

"Well, if you're sure."

"We're sure," I said. "Go on. We're going to need all our energy very soon. And, I promise you, Higashi you won't be disappointed."

She shot me a wistful smile then bade us goodnight.

"You need anything else, Doc?" O'Conner asked after she'd gone.

I flipped the switch terminating the connection. Would the creature return? At that point, I was too tired to speculate. I made some adjustments, aimed the outer lights out further, and got into my sleep position.

Incredible as it may sound, my thoughts drifted not to the extraordinary creature, but to my learned partner in this endeavor, Amaya Higashi. Although we'd worked together for months, I was still taken aback whenever she addressed me by my given name. At first, I'll admit, it made me a little uncomfortable. Lately, however, hearing my name on those soft pink lips was not at all unpleasant.

Yet, that night, my dreams did not include her. I dreamt instead of a lovely young maiden who came to dispel my solitude. Lily-white hands pressed against the porthole. Far-reaching tresses flowed in slow motion framing delicate features. And, emerald eyes sparkled as they delved into the corners of my soul. The elongated tentacles behind her, the delicate webbing between each finger, even the rippling gills beneath her jawline were immaterial. She didn't speak, but I could hear her voice inside my head like the ringing of a distant bell. "Come with me, and I will show you a world more beauteous than you can imagine."

At that moment, another voice tangible and real awakened me.

"Hey, Doc. Can you hear me?"

I jerked up and looked to the porthole. Nothing - just the murky shadows of subaqueous gloom.

"Doc? It's O'Conner. You okay down there?"

God, I detested that man! "I'm here," I spat. My mouth an arid crater, I fumbled for my flask.

"There's a storm brewing. Looks like we might have to haul you up early."

"What? We can't leave now!"

"Don't shoot the messenger, Doc. You know it's not up to me."

"Let me speak to Higashi."

"She's not here. I think she's up on deck."

"Listen to me, you fool! This creature may well be the single most important discovery of our time. Go and find Higashi. *Now!*"

"Okay, okay. Hold on."

I guzzled lukewarm water from my flask and glanced at the clock – 09:45. Damn! Why had I slept so long? Pulling up the latest recordings, I saw nothing but those ghastly white fish flitting across the screen. Then… *there!* He came back! The creature had returned while I was sleeping. Apparently, O'Conner was dozing too, that son of a bitch!

This time, the recording was perfect with hardly a glare. Coming to a halt less than three feet from the porthole, the creature remained there, watching me sleep.

I must admit, as I sat, watching him watching me, I was tempted to call the ship and have them pull me up that very instant. But, my anxiety eased as I realized the significance of this new footage. This was it! This creature was my ticket to immortality!

And, I had proof. Now they'd understand why my research couldn't be cut short.

Where the hell was Higashi?

I poured a dash of water into my palm and swiped it across my face. Personal hygiene wasn't a priority in the construction of this habitat. My olfactory glands were acclimated to the odor, but after going a week without bathing, I was aware that I probably reeked. My first order of business, once freed from this tiny dungeon, was a long hot shower. The second was to fire O'Conner.

I wondered about the storm he had mentioned. It was probably just a little squall. Surely, the captain would agree to hunker down and stay once he saw what I'd discovered.

Unfortunately, Captain Torrence was not a man of science. I'd have to trust Higashi to convince him. Perhaps, if all else failed, she could seduce him with her feminine wiles. She was, after all, an attractive woman. With her jet-black hair and… It was then, I realized that the captivating female from my dream resembled a younger somewhat thinner version of Higashi.

Outside, the sightless fish were back. I was bewildered as to why they kept flocking to my porthole. Once again, it seemed as if those wan flesh-covered eyes were following my every move. I told myself I was being paranoid and that I just needed to focus on *him*.

"I'm here, Dr. Whitman." Higashi's voice rang out. "O'Conner said you wanted to speak with me."

She sounded out of breath. And, she was calling me Doctor Whitman again. This was not a good sign.

"Higashi!" I said. "He came back! Our Pontus has returned. Look, I'll show you."

"What's a pontus?" O'Conner asked.

"Be quiet," Higashi said.

I pressed play.

"Holy shit." Higashi's voice was little more than a whisper.

"What the hell is it?" O'Conner said. "I've never seen anything like *that* before."

"That's rather the point," I said. "Isn't it, Higashi?"

"Fascinating," she said.

"So what's this about a storm?"

"It's a bad one, I'm afraid. Captain Torrence gave orders to terminate the expedition."

"But we can't stop now! You saw the footage. It could be years before we get another opportunity like this. Decades even!"

"I'm sorry, John. I've spoken with the captain, and he's not budging. We have to go."

"No," I said. "I'm sorry, Higashi, but… I'm not coming up. Not yet."

"What do you mean? We have no choice! We signed an agreement to abide by the rules of the captain. Besides, I've seen the reports from NOAA. We're talking possible hurricane here."

"I don't care. Whatever it is, I'll be safer down here anyway."

"But… but, what if we can't get back to you? You only have – "

"I'm staying."

"You can't do this, John! This is crazy!"

Higashi's voice had raised several decibels. Perhaps, she was right. Of course she was right. But, she hadn't seen the creature like I had - face to face.

"Listen to me, Higashi. This creature is like nothing I've ever seen. I can't explain it, but I'm convinced that this animal can be of enormous value to mankind."

"Enormous value to mankind?" I could hear the sarcasm in O'Conner's voice. "Don't you mean, enormous value to you?"

"Shut him up, Higashi! I mean it."

Both she and O'Conner disappeared, but I could hear them arguing off-screen. I couldn't discern most of their dialogue, but I did hear O'Conner say "self-serving prick."

"Okay, he's gone." From the look on Higashi's face, I could tell she was agitated. A part of me felt badly for what I was about to do.

"I'm sorry, Amaya."

Her brown eyes grew wide.

"If they try to pull me up, I'll detach the pod."

"You wouldn't!"

"I would."

"Damn you, John!" With a cry of exasperation, Higashi whirled about and left the room. She'd convince them. They wouldn't dare leave without me.

I terminated the connection. My stomach rumbled, and I realized that I couldn't remember when I'd last eaten. As I leaned down to access the food rations, I noticed how depleted they were. My craft held what I required for two weeks. No more.

I fished a granola bar out of the compartment. As I bit into the chewy morsel, my hunger awoke and I reached for another. When I turned back to the porthole, I couldn't see anything, not even the fish. I looked to the camera on the opposite side of the vessel. The views were indistinguishable from one another - a bleak sunless world with its constant flow of fish droppings and decomposing sea life. Sometimes, it felt as if I was sitting in the bottom of the world's toilet.

Giving up, I leaned back in my chair and allowed my mind to wander. I envisioned the lovely personage from my dream and the look on her face as she smiled at me. I shook my head. This was absurd! I forced my thoughts to our real flesh and blood specimen. Were there more of them? There must be. There had to be!

A red light flashed, indicating that the ship was attempting to contact me. I took my time answering it. When the monitor came into focus, it was neither Higashi nor Captain Torrence. O'Conner, his stupid face filling the screen, was grinning at me.

"Dr. Whitman?"

As if it could be anyone else. "Yes, O'Conner. What do you want?"

"Higashi says that you won't be joining us for the return trip. That true?"

"I'm not discussing this with you. Where is Captain Torrence?"

"He's a little busy right now."

"What about Higashi?"

"She's busy too. It's just you and me now, Doc." O'Conner's grin widened.

I gritted my teeth. "Okay then listen to me, you worthless cretin. We are on the verge of an *unprecedented* discovery here."

"So, you refuse to resurface. Correct?"

I took a deep breath. "Yes! I refuse! To hell with the storm! We've weathered out storms before. This animal could be the biggest finding of the century – maybe even of all time. Don't you want to be part of that?"

"Who me – the worthless cretin? Nah. I prefer life. You see, Doc, the storm is much worse than they thought. And, it's definitely headed this way. Captain Torrence ordered me to either haul your ass up or detach the pod. So… See ya on the other side, Doc."

O'Conner winked and disappeared. As I stared, openmouthed, the screen turned gray. The lights dimmed. I looked to the control panel - "pod detached". They were leaving me! The bastards were actually leaving me behind! I smashed my fist into the console sending a burning pain all the way up my arm.

"To hell with you!" I shouted, my voice reverberating inside the tiny chamber. "To hell with you all!"

It took a while for the gravity of what had just happened to sink in. Not only was I cut off from the outside world, I had no possible way of knowing how long the storm would last. I did some calculations and was horrified to discover that, with my lifeline to the ship now severed, I had just enough oxygen to reach the surface. Storm or no storm, I had to rise immediately.

Had O'Conner realized that? I wasn't just going to fire him. I was going to *destroy* him!

I cannot describe how I felt when the submersible refused to budge.

Raving and cursing, I tried again and again. After a time, I forced myself to calm down and try to troubleshoot the problem. But, I'm a scientist not a mechanic. What if the ship didn't come back? Or, more likely, what if it came too late?

I accessed the remainder of my food stores and shoved them in my mouth until it felt as if I would explode. It seems that we, as human beings, often resort to self-destructive behavior in times of stress. With no access to alcohol or cigarettes, food was all I had left.

Afterward, I turned off the lights and stared out at the gloom.

That's when I saw him. The creature was there, swimming back and forth just beyond my lights. Had he been there all along? A sort of madness took me. "This is *your* fault, you son of a bitch!" I shouted, raising a fist to the porthole.

As if in response to my tirade, he came to a full stop. Then slowly and deliberately, he drifted closer. The moment his eyes locked onto mine, I realized my mistake. My first instinct was correct. This was no ordinary animal or a specimen to be scrutinized. This was a horrific monster bent on dragging me with him through the entrails of the earth!

When the loathsome beast was within inches of the glass, I lowered myself to the floor, crawled into a ball, and wept.

After a while, I looked up to see that he'd gone.

That was hours ago. Since then, I've lain huddled, like a rabbit in its burrow, reminiscing - recalling the things I've accomplished and regretting the things I did not. When it's over and done with, who's to say what's really important in these limited blocks of time life allots us.

I thought of all the friendships I'd let slip away. I thought of my mother, dead for twenty-some years. I thought of Higashi. I realize now that she cared for me and I for her. I wonder how she reacted when they left me behind. Was she in agreement? I think not. I only wish I could've told her goodbye.

The air is getting thinner now. The last time I dared to look, the phantom fish had returned. One by one, they were converging on my porthole. I no longer doubt that they can see me. Perhaps the black devil has returned to taunt me as well. As much as I don't want to, I have to look.

Positioning myself in front of the porthole, I flip on the outer light. I gasp aloud as my heart falters inside my chest. For a split-second, I see the dreaded monstrosity leering at me. Then I realize it's not him after all. It's the beautiful maiden from my dream.

I close my eyes and count to ten. When I open them she's still there, a mischievous smile tugging at her lips. What a fool I was to think she resembled Higashi. No mere mortal could compare to this fair being.

She motions for me to open the porthole.

No, dear one. I cannot.

She is persistent. I try, but I can't look away from those dark, soulful eyes. They speak to me of an underwater paradise. They promise peace, happiness, immortality. She beckons with her dainty hand while serenading me inside my head with a soft lilting voice.

Perhaps I won't perish. Perhaps only this rancid-smelling carcass will cease to exist, and I will be free to swim alongside her exploring these vast limitless waters forever.

Wait! When did I unlock the porthole? I was not aware I had done so.

Those eyes – I can't escape them. She wants me. She *needs* me.

My hand reaches for the latch…

CHAPTER 3

Peg frowned as she placed the book back on the table. That poor man. Pushing the disturbing scene from her mind, she was thinking about rejoining the others when she saw her hostess approaching. Eyes bright with amusement and drink, Sasha was carrying two more glasses.

"Hey, sexxxy lady," she slurred. "Mind if I join you?"

Without waiting for a reply, she handed over both glasses and pulled an empty lounge chair next to Peg's. "Having fun?"

"Of course." Peg forced a smile. "I really appreciate the invite, Sasha."

"No problem," Sasha said, relieving her of one of the glasses. "I know what it's like to be the new girl in town. Hey, you met Ryan yet?"

Sasha nodded toward a man Peg had not yet noticed. Thick blonde hair with muscles rippling beneath a skintight polo, his head was tilted back in laughter. Peg gasped. Although obviously in better shape, Ryan's resemblance to her ex-boyfriend Jake was uncanny.

"I hear he's currently available." Sasha winked.

"No thanks." Peg sneered. A Jake look-alike was the last thing she needed. "It's those short, bald, nerdy types that get me hot," she said.

"You're hilarious!" Sasha snorted. Settling into her chair, she took a sip from her drink then leaned back regarding Peg through half-closed eyes.

Seconds passed, and Peg understood that it was now her turn to hold up the conversation. She sifted through her weary brain for something to talk about, taking a swig from her own glass to stall for time. Of course! The news update she'd seen on the break room television earlier that day was not exactly amusing but it was, at least, newsworthy.

"Oh my God!" Peg began, raising her voice for emphasis. "Have you seen the news? That wealthy couple the Whitmans were acquitted today. Can you believe it?"

Eyes bulging, Sasha jerked upright and coughed wetly, apparently having taken too large a drink.

She seemed okay however, so Peg kept going. "I mean, the evidence against them was overwhelming, and you could just tell by looking at that bitch-face wife of his that she was guilty."

Sasha, her face now bright red, lunged forward and grabbed Peg's arm. "Quiet," she hissed. "They'll hear you!"

"Who?" Peg asked. "Who will hear me?"

"The Whitmans. Don't - "

But, Peg had already swiveled around in her chair. Sure enough, seated at a table directly behind them was the ill-famed couple whose faces had been plastered across every TV screen in America for months. Dark and petite, it was Macushla Whitman one noticed first. Though plain and nondescript with her drab floor-length dresses and her long black hair pulled back in a knot, she drew attention like a full moon draws the tide. She was facing the other way, so Peg looked to Mr. Whitman. A tall, painfully thin man with silver hair and mustache, his glasses reflected the light that shimmered atop the pool.

Was he looking at her? Peg couldn't tell. She scooted her chair even closer to Sasha's. "What are *they* doing here?"

"Brad's brother used to work for Mr. Whitman," Sasha said, fanning herself with a napkin. "You know Whitman's an accomplished Marine Biologist, right?"

"He is?"

Sasha nodded. "He's written tons of books."

Peg frowned. "Well, what's he doing in Ohio then? Last time I checked, it was quite a jog from here to the Atlantic."

Sasha rested her elbow on the arm of Peg's chair. "There are different opinions on that," she whispered. "But, regardless of why they're here, Brad says they're actually a very nice couple who were just trying to help those poor unfortunate women. Apparently, the whole thing backfired in their faces."

Peg felt her own face getting hot. *Now you've done it.*

"I'm so sorry, Sasha. I had no idea they were friends of yours."

"It's okay. To tell you the truth, they kind'a give me the willies."

"Well, what does Whitman do now?" Peg asked.

"I dunno. I think they own a string of restaurants or something." Sasha scooted up to the edge of her chair. "Listen, hon. I need to go inside and check on the buffet. Wanna come?"

Peg tilted her head in the Whitman's direction. "Do you think they heard what I said?"

"I doubt it. The music's pretty loud out here. So, you coming? We've got shrimp cocktail, stuffed mushrooms, oh and some nummy chocolate cheesecake."

Peg's pulse quickened at the mention of cheesecake, but the pressure of her little black skirt against her belly reminded her that she was supposed to be dieting.

"No thanks. Maybe later."

"Okay." Sasha pointed to an open set of patio doors set back beneath the arches. "It's straight through there if you change your mind." She emptied her glass and got to her feet.

"Hey, Sasha?" Peg plucked the book off the table.

"Yes?"

"Is this yours?"

Sasha squinted at the object in Peg's hand. "Nope, never seen it before." With that, she disappeared into the throng leaving Peg on her own once more.

Leaning back, Peg nursed the drink Sasha had given her. How much longer would she have to wait until someone showed her to a bedroom? After embarrassing herself by unwittingly insulting her host's guests, Peg didn't feel inclined to talk to anyone else. And, there was no way she could drive home now. Her body felt weighted, and her eyelids were starting to droop again. She imagined herself falling backward onto a huge downy-soft mattress.

A bright peal of laughter made her jump. Had she nodded off? Peg adjusted herself in the chair, placed the icy glass against her forehead, and willed herself to stay awake.

Moments later, she became aware of a baseless, yet certain, knowledge that she was being watched. Placing her glass on the table, she leaned down for her purse. As she straightened back up, Peg glanced over to see if the Whitmans were still there.

They were there all right! Only this time, instead of looking the other way, Mrs. Whitman was staring directly at her. Their eyes met, and Peg felt something deep inside herself recoil. She swallowed hard and forced her lips into a smile.

But, Macushla did not return the smile. Instead she gave Peg a look of pure hatred.

Peg's heart fluttered. She wanted to look away, but as Macushla's keen eyes bored into hers, she found that she was unable to move or even to blink. Seconds became minutes as she sat gawking at the couple like a simpleton, her body stationary as if somehow suspended in time. *I can't stop. I can't fucking stop!*

In the background, the disc jockey played an old Blue Oyster Cult song. Peg had often listened to the tune; in fact it was one of her favorites. This time, however, something about it sounded wrong. The words were jumbled together, and there was an extra voice, a female voice, that hadn't been there before. *But, she's not really singing. It's more like... humming.*

Eerie and surreal, the voice intertwined with the music then slowly drowned it out until the humming was all that Peg could hear. Louder and louder it grew, twirling and swirling inside her brain.

"Miss? You okay, Miss?"

Peg felt as if she was falling from some great dizzying height. She reached out and grabbed the table with both hands, dropping her purse and spilling its contents onto the patio.

"Allow me," someone said.

Head spinning, Peg watched as a stranger dropped to his knees and began shoving her compact, phone, and tampons back into her purse. "Did you hear something weird just now?" she muttered, still clutching the table.

"Weird? Like what?"

"Like... Never mind."

"I didn't hear anything, Miss. I just thought you looked a little er... discombobulated."

When the man stood up, Peg took note of his short stature, receding hairline, and thick-lensed glasses and was reminded of the snide comment she'd made to Sasha earlier. *Well here he is - Mr. Right.* She smirked.

Mistaking her expression for one of gratitude, the stranger beamed at her warmly and introduced himself.

But, Peg wasn't listening. Body tense, she imagined she could feel Macushla's eyes, still boring into her back. Maybe this was a good time to go and meet the distinguished Dr. Carlson. Swallowing hard, she thrust out her hand.

"Peg Starling. Nice to meet you. I was just about to go inside. Would you care to join me?"

"I'd love too." Grinning, the stranger helped her to her feet.

"So..." Peg began, suddenly feeling the need for small talk. "Do you know Dr. Carlson well?"

"Let's just say we have... similar interests."

When they reached the arches, it appeared that everyone had the same idea at once and were now swarming toward the patio doors like bees toward a hive. As Peg and her companion squeezed through, she realized with embarrassment that, not only was she still holding his hand, she was clasping it much tighter than necessary. Loosening her grip, she pretended to bump into someone so that she could pull free.

The room they entered was massive with bright lights and warm bodies pressed close. Striking a pose beside a long generously laden buffet, Sasha looked over and waved. Was that Dr. Carlson beside her? Yes. Peg recognized his big cube-shaped head. Thinking she should freshen up before meeting him, she abandoned her dwarfish sidekick and went in search of a bathroom.

After relieving herself, Peg leaned over the sink to examine her reflection. "Why are you still here?" she asked the wan image in the mirror. "You know damn well that what you really want is to go home and veg out in front of the TV." Having sobered up since her bizarre encounter with the Whitmans, Peg decided that was exactly what she was going to do. She could meet Dr. Carlson some other time.

She emerged from the bathroom to find her Good Samaritan waiting for her in the hallway. *Crap!* Should she risk insulting another of Sasha and Dr. Carlson's guests? Probably not. Besides, the hunger pangs in her belly were beginning to overpower her resolve. Maybe she could stay just a little while longer.

"Feeling better?" the man asked, peering up at her. "I took the liberty of getting us a plate."

Peg followed him to a table set with two plates filled with a variety of tempting hors d'oeuvres. *So much for that diet.* Mouth watering, Peg selected a dainty looking cracker topped with cheese. She was about to pop it in her mouth when she noticed something lying to the left of her plate.

"Where did that come from?" Peg nodded toward the book.

The man looked surprised. "I assumed it was yours. You were clutching it to your chest, but you dropped it when we came inside."

"I was? Peg stared at the dark rectangular object. Was it her imagination, or did the book look a little bigger than before? Seeing it, reminded her of the poor man left to die alone in the depths of the ocean. *It's just fiction, silly.*

"May I?" the stranger asked, eyeing the book with interest.

"Knock yourself out."

Peg watched as he picked up the book and examined it. Should she ask his name? No. It was too late now. She'd be leaving soon anyway.

As he began to read aloud, Peg lowered the cracker back onto her plate.

CHAPTER 4
The Swing Set

When asked, I sometimes say that I am an only child. That's not exactly true. I once had an older sister who disappeared when we were young. When I say disappeared, I mean that in the literal sense.

I was seven when my parents separated for the first time. My sister, Rachel, was eight. I'm not sure of the circumstances leading to the break up, but I think it had something to do with Daddy losing his job at the steel mill. Instead of kicking him out, Momma, Rachel, and I moved in with Aunt Jane and her three obnoxious children. We soon discovered that living with relatives is a less than desirable situation.

After a time, someone told Momma of an affordable (dirt-cheap) place that we could rent. Way back from the road amidst a cluster of trees, the abandoned home had been neglected for years. This did not discourage my mother. With a scarf round her head and rubber gloves on her hands, she could turn any pigsty into a palace.

There are things, however, no amount of cleansing can purge.

I remember the first time we explored the old house, me clinging to Momma's skirt while my sister, wide-eyed and laughing, darted from room to room. Momma and I were still in the parlor when Rachel let out an excited yip and ran back to grab my arm.

"Come look, Julie!" she cried. "You'll never guess what's in the backyard!"

It was a tired looking swing set.

As soon as we moved in, Rachel begged to play on the swings, but our mother forbade it, declaring the "rickety contraption" unsafe and the weed-choked yard thick with ticks, snakes, and poison ivy. Rachel tried pouting then crying to no avail. As for me, I was too frightened of the jungle-like yard to care.

It was summertime and school was out, so Momma handed us some coloring books and told us to stay out of the way. The rambling house had at least four bedrooms, but as my sister and I were close, we preferred to bunk together. We chose a wide, airy room overlooking the backyard, and after Momma changed the sheets on our new queen-sized bed, I plopped down and began to color. Still pouting, Rachel pulled a chair up to the window and sat gazing out at the swing set.

Days passed in much the same way with Momma cleaning, Rachel pouting, and me entertaining myself. Then Daddy showed up, and after some grownup words between him and Momma, they made up, and we were a family once more.

As he still didn't have a job, Daddy set to work around the house. His first task, per Rachel's request, was to clear out the backyard and repair the old swing set. When at last, we were permitted to go out and play, I suddenly took ill and was sent to bed. Fearing I was contagious, Momma prepared a separate room for Rachel, and I was left to suffer alone.

Of course, it wasn't as bad as I make it sound. My parents checked in on me often. Daddy would sit on the edge of my bed and play cards or read to me while Momma took my temperature and brought me bowls of homemade soup. I enjoyed the extra attention, but I missed my sister terribly. As soon as no one was looking, I'd slide out of bed and tiptoe to the chair beside the window. Rachel was always outside and she was always doing the same thing – swinging. The swing set also had a slide and a bar you could do flips on, but Rachel seemed to prefer the swings. I also noticed that she always used the swing on the right, never the one on the left.

On the third or maybe the fourth day, I saw that Rachel had ceased swinging and was pretending to have a conversation with someone in the swing beside her. She's making believe it's me, I thought with a smile. Hearing footsteps on the stair, I hopped back into bed.

That evening, when I resumed my seat by the window, I saw something that chilled me to the core. Rachel was swinging, as usual, while beside her the other swing was moving back and forth *all by itself!*

She's been pushing it, I thought. It'll slow down any minute now. But, it didn't. And after watching for several minutes, I observed that, although she smiled at it from time to time, Rachel never once touched the other swing.

I can't remember getting to my feet, but I must have because seconds later I was out on the upstairs landing screaming for my parents. Momma ran up and grabbed me then carried me back to bed. I told her what I'd seen, but instead of looking out the window, she placed her palm across my forehead. "You're burning up," she said and left the room. She came back with some medicine, I recognized as bitter tasting, and insisted that I take it.

After that, I fell asleep and didn't wake up until the next day. With the early morning sunlight streaming through my window, I convinced myself that what I'd witnessed in the yard below was part of a fever-induced dream. When Daddy appeared with my breakfast tray, I didn't mention it.

Sometime later, finding myself alone again, I got out of bed and walked to the window. I looked down into the yard and my heart leapt into my throat. This time, not only was the swing beside Rachel swaying back and forth, but it appeared that someone, or some *thing* was occupying it. It reminded me of colors reflected on a soap bubble, only it was much larger and in the shape of a child. As I stared at it, mesmerized, my head began to throb, and my legs wobbled beneath me. The sun slipped behind the clouds, and I lost sight of it.

Minutes passed as I kept my post by the window, waiting for the sun to reappear. All of a sudden, Rachel straightened her legs and came to a halt. The swing beside her stopped as well. I still couldn't see the apparition, and I might've been able to convince myself that it wasn't real if not for one thing - Rachel was leaning toward the other swing, talking to someone.

I jumped back, stumbled, and nearly fell, onto the hard wood floor. I wanted to scream, I wanted to hide, I wanted to crawl back under the covers and stay there forever. But, she was my sister. I returned to the window and grabbed hold of the sash, intending to shout down to Rachel. But, though I pulled and strained, my nails digging painfully into the wood, the old window wouldn't budge. What's more, the sudden motion had sent the room spinning around me while my breakfast churned in my stomach. Giving up, I made my way back to the bed.

As my head began to clear, I contemplated what I'd seen and what I should do about it. If I called for my parents, all it would get me was more of that horrible tasting medicine. I needed to talk to Rachel. But how? The window was painted shut, and my parents wouldn't allow her in the same room with me.

I decided to write her a note. Pulling the back off one of my coloring books, I scribbled a message asking her to sneak into my room. I didn't trust Momma to give it to Rachel without reading it, so I decided to wait for Dad.

That afternoon, the sky turned dreary, and it was Momma who brought my lunch. It was also she who returned later for my tray.

"Where's Daddy?" I asked.

"Your guess is as good as mine." She frowned.

As soon as Momma left, I returned to my chair. What I saw then might've been unexceptional, if not for what I'd seen before. Sitting in the swing alongside my sister was a young, dark-haired girl. Because of the distance, I couldn't quite make out her features, but what I couldn't help but notice, was that she appeared to be soaking wet. Hair drenched and dripping, the dress she wore clung to her slight frame like a second skin. She and my sister talked for a moment, then they both began to swing. Higher and higher they went, their skinny legs stretching out and tucking back in unison. Meanwhile, my headache returned with a painful pounding, which seemed to coincide with every swing.

I stood up and pressed my forehead against the cool glass. The pain increased, and I was having trouble keeping the girls in focus. Were they really moving that fast?

As I continued to watch, their bodies became bleary as if they, or I, were underwater. I thought it was just the headache affecting my vision until I realized that the rest of the swing set, the trees, and everything surrounding the two girls were clear and well defined. That horrid girl was fading away and she was taking my sister with her!

I tried to scream, but fear constricted my throat. In desperation, I pounded my fists against the window. The glass shattered into a thousand pieces; then I heard Daddy's voice behind me. "Julie! What the hell?"

The next thing I remember, I was lying in his arms and Momma was pressing something cool against my forehead.

I never saw my sister again. I'll never forget hearing my parents call her name out in the yard, and the way their voices grew shrill with panic. I tried to tell them what I'd witnessed through the window, but no one lends credence to a seven-year-old spouting absurdities.

Due to the stress, I had what my mother called "a setback" where, instead of getting well, my symptoms returned with a vengeance. For days, I did not leave my bed, nor did I see either of my parents. Instead, my aunt and some lady from the church brought my meals and cared for me.

When I was better, my parents told me with red-rimmed eyes that Rachel had wandered off and gotten lost. I later learned that the woods around our house were thoroughly searched and a nearby gravel pit dredged of its contents. Some say my sister was abducted. As hard as it is to accept, I suppose this must be true.

After a time, you see, I realized that the memory was a product of my illness and imagination. What else could it be?

Still, I'm a mother myself now with two beautiful children Faith, who's nine, and Lucas, who's seven. And, although my husband thinks me ridiculous, to this day, neither of them has been permitted to play on a swing set.

CHAPTER 5

As her Good Samaritan closed the book, Peg realized that she'd been sitting, elbows on the table, enthralled in the story. She'd always felt cheated, having had two brothers and no sisters. But, apparently, it could've been worse. Having a sister and then losing her had to be heart wrenching.

"That's weird," she said. "That's not the same story I read. Let me see that."

"Of course." The man placed the book in her hand.

Before she could wrap her fingers around it, Peg felt a familiar chill along her spine. Turning instinctively, she spotted Mr. and Mrs. Whitman, glowering at her from across the room. Surely, they hadn't followed her inside… Had they?

"That's it!" Releasing the book, Peg grabbed her purse instead. "I'm outta here!" Without waiting for a response, she got up and began shoving her way through the crowd.

She was almost to the door when Ryan, the Jake look-a-like, stepped in front of her holding out a glass of lime green liquid. "Sasha said you like these." He smiled, charm wafting from his body like steam from a hot bath.

Flustered, Peg accepted the glass. *Ah, what the hell.* She downed it in one gulp and handed it back.

"Wow!" Ryan remarked. "Sasha was right."

"Thanks," Peg said, and bolted through the door.

The air outside felt cooler than before, and the wind had started to pick up making Peg wish that she'd brought along a wrap. *It doesn't matter. It'll be warm in the car.*

After weaving through another horde of bodies, she sprinted back through the latticed tunnel and across the driveway, her heels skating dangerously on the slippery cobbles. It was then, she spotted a SUV parked sideways at the end of the drive, effectively blocking everyone else in. "Son of a bitch!" Peg glanced back at the house. It would be nearly impossible to find the owner amongst all those drunken partiers. *And,* she'd have to face that horrid couple again!

Weighing the possibilities, it occurred to her that she could get out by driving through a section of the yard. After making sure no one was watching, Peg jumped in her car and started the engine. "Sorry, Sasha," she whispered, as she plowed an ugly path across their immaculate front lawn. Upon reaching the road, she backed her car off to the side, put it in park, and set the navigation system for home. Seconds later, "5 hrs. 57 min." flashed across the screen. "What the hell?"

It was then, Peg remembered that, according its most recent settings, "Home" was still in Divinity, Kentucky. With that realization, a vision emerged unbidden, from her memory. It was of Jake, sitting on the front porch of the little house they had rented together on Fifth Street. He and his coonhound, Sam, used to wait there for her every evening when she got off work. Even those nights when she got held up at the restaurant covering for someone else, they were always there, waiting.

How could things have gone so very wrong? Peg swiped a bitter tear from her cheek. She made the necessary adjustments to the GPS and pulled back onto the road.

Heading for home at last, she noticed that some other people, who'd parked beside the curb, were leaving early too. She reduced her speed, swiveling her head to see if she recognized them.

Peg felt a sobering jolt. Mr. and Mrs. Whitman were getting into a dark gray sedan. Whitman was holding the door for his wife while she attempted to slide inside, her legs, no doubt, entangled in her unfashionably long skirt.

"Oh God!" Peg gasped. "They're leaving too?" She punched the accelerator, intending to put as much distance between herself and the creepy twosome as possible.

Peg hadn't gone far, however, when she saw flashing lights in her rearview mirror. "Damn it!" She tightened her grip on the steering wheel and pulled to the side. Grabbing her purse, she reached in for her driver's license and a breath mint to mask her alcohol-tainted breath. As her groping hand fumbled around, it brushed against something cool and smooth. *It can't be.*

Peg pulled the book out and flung it into the floor. How the hell did it get inside her purse? Did whatshisname put it there when she wasn't looking? He must have. But… Peg thought back to some fifteen minutes earlier. Her hand was on the book when she noticed the Whitmans staring at her from across the room. She had immediately let go of the book, grabbed her purse, and made for the door. It just didn't make sense.

After relinquishing her license, registration, and insurance card to the patrolman, Peg sat back and fumed while he returned to his cruiser.

Now, she was going to get her first-ever speeding ticket, and it was all because of that odious woman and her creepy husband.

As if in response to her thoughts, the gray sedan suddenly pulled up alongside Peg's vehicle. She turned to see Macushla glaring at her through the passenger side window. Eyes like tiny slits, her seemingly over-wide mouth was twisted into a malicious scowl. Avoiding her gaze, Peg looked in the rearview mirror and silently prayed for the policeman to return. After a few moments, the sedan sped up and drove away. *Those people are insane.*

Despite what she'd told Sasha, Peg wasn't really familiar with the specifics of the Whitman trial. Since the patrolman had yet to return, she retrieved her phone and began searching for more information. What Peg did know was that it had all started because of some missing women… illegal immigrants. Yes, that was it. As she stared into the tiny screen, the notorious saga began to unfold.

The first hit stated that, although enough evidence had been unearthed to indict the Whitmans, in the end, a conviction had proven impossible. It further stated that this was largely due to the fact that none of the missing women were ever found. Scrolling down, Peg learned of a teenage girl who, months prior, burst into a local police station half dressed and hysterical. After making some outlandish statements regarding the Whitmans, she ran back into the street and vanished. The young woman's outburst was in Spanish, but luckily, a Spanish-speaking clerical worker had overheard the girl's ravings was able to translate to the officers on duty. Human trafficking was suspected and an investigation launched immediately. The results linked the wealthy but reclusive Whitmans to the disappearance of several women who were rumored to have entered the country illegally. Their families had, understandably, refrained from alerting the authorities for fear of having their loved ones deported.

"Friends of yours?" The patrolman leaned down to return Peg's driver's license.

Startled, she jumped in her seat. For a moment, she didn't understand the question. Then Peg realized that the officer must've seen the Whitman's pull up beside her. "Not exactly," she said, accepting the card from his outstretched hand.

The officer provided a brief explanation of the citation. "Drive safe now." He gave her car an authoritative smack and walked away.

Peg started her car but hesitated before pulling back into the street. Just how crazy were those people? Was it possible they could be waiting for her somewhere further up the road? She stayed put until the patrol car was out of sight then, making a tight U-turn, proceeded in the opposite direction. She could find another way home.

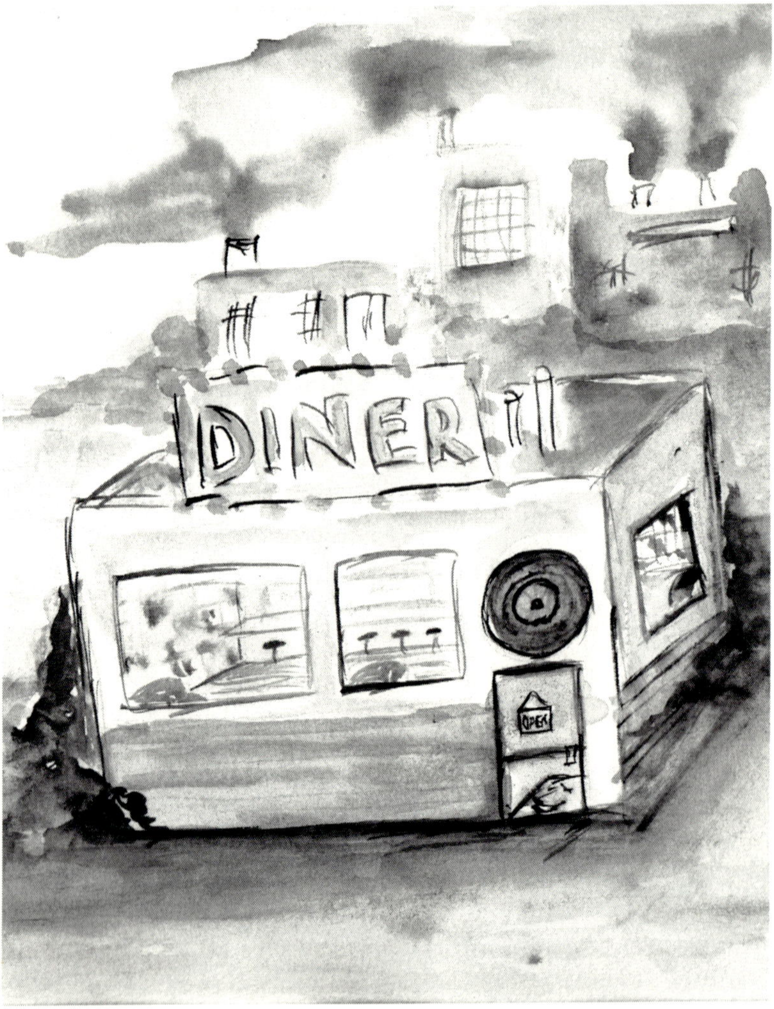
DINER
OPEN

CHAPTER 6

Some time later, a rumbling in her stomach reminded Peg that she hadn't eaten since lunchtime the day before. She'd left the party at just past midnight, and the handful of restaurants she passed were already closed. Even more disturbing, was the fact that her GPS was acting stupid. "Recalculating… Recalculating," it chimed. The wretched thing had directed her through several little podunk towns, the last being some ten miles back, and now it had lost its mind completely. Where the hell was she?

The road ahead was a straight black line, at the side of which, Peg saw only fields with the occasional darkened farmhouse, ramshackle barn, or tumbledown silo. With the full moon gleaming like a giant celestial nightlight, she imagined that everyone in the entire world was fast asleep. And, oh how she longed to join them.

Peg flipped on the radio and dialed through the stations. Static… "He stopped loving her today," static… "Can't live without you…" She flipped it off again. Gritting her teeth, she tried to dispel the image of Jake the music had instilled in her mind. *It's over. Deal with it!*

All at once, she realized that the two-lane road she'd been following was widening into a four-lane thoroughfare. Wiping her eyes, she focused on a bleary image in the distance. At last! She was coming to a town.

As she drew near, Peg's enthusiasm waned then disappeared altogether. Although the buildings were large and numerous, they showed no signs of life - abandoned factories she realized. With broken windows and crumbling edifices, they loomed over her car like forgotten monsters, frightening, yet pitiable at the same time.

Peg was about to despair when she spotted a small, brightly lit diner. In the middle of nowhere, it was like finding an oasis in the desert. "Oh *please* be open", she whispered, slowing the car. Just then, three women in black leather jackets filed out of the diner, each one clutching a paper sack.

"Jackpot!"

Peg veered toward the parking lot before realizing that there were several long strands of yellow caution tape barring the way. A makeshift sign nailed to a post stated that the lot was being repaved and instructed all patrons to park across the street in the old factory parking lot. It was followed by a brief apology for the inconvenience.

"Damned inconvenient, I'd say!" Peg looked around uncertainly. As she sat, both hands on the wheel, the three women strode past, chatting animatedly over their bulging paper sacks. *I'll bet there's something yummy in those bags*, Peg thought. Maybe she could get directions *and* grab a bite to eat. She backed up and swung her car into the capacious lot on the other side of the road. With the exception of three Harleys the women were heading toward, the only other vehicle on the lot was a large, windowless van.

Peg chose a spot well away from the van then sat peering out at the gigantic asphalt sea surrounding her. Why did they have to leave it like this? If they weren't going to use the land anymore, couldn't they tear the factories down so that Mother Nature could reclaim her space? Peg shook her head. Sometimes she felt ashamed to be human.

Gathering her courage, she got out of the car and sprinted toward the diner. Big glass windows coated inside with a layer of steam made the restaurant's interior appear hazy and dreamlike. When she got closer, Peg tried to see if anyone was inside, but all she could make out were some empty booths and the elongated edge of a counter top. Nevertheless, the sign on the door said "Open" so she hastily skirted around one side of the lot taking care not to step on the freshly laid pavement.

It wasn't until her fingers clasped round the handle that Peg caught sight of the restaurant's solitary occupant. Dressed all in white, he was removing a small chef's hat as he emerged from behind the counter. Peg hopped inside and winced as a tiny bell above her head announced her arrival.

The somewhat stocky fellow, who looked as if he hadn't shaved in days, stopped short. "Sorry Ma'am, I was just fixin to close up."

Peg's entire body slumped in defeat. Then, as the lingering smell of fried food titillated her nostrils, she decided that she wasn't giving up that easily. "Oh no," she said, attempting to look pitiful. "I've been lost for over an hour now, and I am *so* hungry."

In truth, Peg had only been driving for twenty minutes, at most. Watching the man's expression, she hoped that her rash exaggeration wouldn't make her seem dishonest. Just as she hoped, a compassionate look crossed his face as he stood, hat in hand, wavering.

"Please," she said. "I'm not picky. I'd probably even eat your hat there if you dipped it in chocolate first."

With that, the man chuckled and plopped the hat back on his head. "All right, sweetheart. Come on in, I think I gotta clean one round here somewhere."

"Thank you!" Peg hopped aboard the closest stool before he could change his mind.

"The pop machine's down for cleanin," the man said, resuming his place behind the counter. "An I dumped out the lasta' the coffee so it'll have to be milk er water."

"Milk please."

"The grill's off too, so there ain't much to choose from. I got some salads over there in the fridge and there's a couple loose-meat sandwiches left over."

Peg hesitated. A salad would be the better choice. But… "Loose-meat sandwiches?"

"Best in the state." His blue eyes twinkled.

Despite his gruff, slightly unkempt appearance, Peg decided he was kind of cute when he smiled. *That's just your stomach talking, dummy.* "Loose-meat sandwich it is!"

Her amiable host nodded, and a clump of dark curls escaped from beneath his hat onto his weather beaten forehead. He deftly replaced them and poured her a glass of milk. He then produced a thin, oblong package from the display cooler, loosened the paper, and popped it into the microwave. "They're better fresh," he said apologetically.

"I'm sure it's fine." Peg took a gulp of ice-cold milk. As it mixed with the alcohol in her stomach, she thought for a second that she was going to be sick.

"You all right, sweetheart?" the nice man asked.

"I'm okay," she mumbled, covering her mouth with a napkin.

"Well, what's your name then?"

"Peg. What's yours?"

"Name's Frances, but ever'body round here calls me Mac."

"I guess you do look more like a Mac," she said, watching him remove his grease-splattered apron. A plain white t-shirt clung to his body, revealing tight abs below a wide, muscular chest.

"Thanks, I guess," he said, looking away.

"You're not from around here. Are you?" Peg asked.

"Me? Nah. I'm from a little place in Kentucky you prob'ly never heard of. It's called called Blaze."

"Blaze? Really? We were practically neighbors then! I'm from Divinity." Peg was surprised by the flood of emotions welling up inside her - delight, nostalgia, homesickness. Homesickness?

Mac squinted at her suspiciously. "You shittin me?"

Peg laughed and held up one hand, palm side out. "Born and raised."

"Well, don't that beat all! You sure don't sound like no briar-hopper."

"Yeah, well you know." She hung her head. "Just trying to fit in."

A minute later, she bit into the best sandwich she'd ever tasted. "Oh my God! What's *in* this?"

"Secret recipe," Mac said with a wink. "I could tell ya, but then I'd haf'ta kill ya."

"Might be worth it," Peg countered and took another bite.

Mac chuckled. He grabbed the milk jug and topped off her glass before returning it to the fridge.

Her eyes on Mac's backside, Peg thought about asking him for directions, but it occurred to her to try the Maps application on her phone first. Just because her car's navigation system was screwed up, didn't mean that her phone's would be too. Holding the sandwich in one hand, she began pulling stuff out of her purse with the other.

"Shit!" Peg exclaimed, and then choked on the bite of sandwich still in her mouth. Standing up, she took a gulp of milk and swallowed hard.

"What's the matter?" Mac asked, his eyes filled with concern.

Peg remained standing as she stared in horror at the little book now lying on the counter.

"That… that stupid, fucking book!" Using the butt of her hand, she shoved it across the counter. "It's like it's following me or something."

Mac tilted his head, a wry grin playing at the corners of his mouth. "A *book* is following you."

"I know it sounds crazy. But, I swear to God, I threw that thing in the floor of my car a little while ago. I haven't touched it since."

"This, I gotta see." Mac plucked the book off the counter and started reading it to her.

Yvonne T. Tibbs

CHAPTER 7
Deirdre

Dear Dr. Simon,

I hope you are well. First, I must apologize for leaving without saying goodbye. I know it's inexcusable after everything you've done for me. I just had to get away. I'm living in San Diego now. With its gorgeous beaches, free-spirited people, and exhilarating nightlife, Southern California is everything I hoped it would be.

You'll be pleased to learn that I took your advice and went back to nursing school. You were right. Once I got my head on straight, it wasn't hard at all. I'm finally here, living the life I've always dreamed of, and I owe it all to you.

But, for me, it seems heartache is always just resting up for its next big pounce. Something dreadful has happened, doctor, and, as usual, I'm running to you for solace. I met a wonderful young woman named Iris in nursing school. I'm not sure what drew us together initially, but we soon became inseparable. With her long blonde hair, emerald eyes, and infectious laugh, Iris was popular on campus. Academically, however, she was inept. We used to study together after class, and she relied on me heavily. I'm ashamed to say it, but sometimes I even completed her assignments for her. I know it was wrong, but I couldn't just stand by and watch her fail. Iris was so vibrant and carefree. Just being around her was a joy.

After graduation, we both got jobs at Bainbridge Memorial, so we decided to rent an apartment together. Months passed, and everything seemed to be going great. I had no idea she was so unhappy. I guess it's true what they say, that you can never truly know someone. We delude ourselves into thinking we understand those closest to us when, truth is, we barely even know ourselves.

I'm sorry, Doctor. I've drifted off subject, and I'm sure you're anxious to know the reason for this letter. Last night, I found my poor, sweet Iris in the bathtub - her delicate wrists sliced to ribbons.

Just yesterday morning we sat together, here at this very table. She with her juice and I with my coffee, we munched on day-old donuts and talked about work. Well, I was talking about work. Iris was going on and on about the Richmonds again.

You see, Iris's aunt works for that actress Lauren Richmond. She plays Vanessa Stone on the soap opera "Stone Pillows." Anyway, Lauren and her husband, Xavier, have two daughters. The eldest is diabetic and the little one has asthma, so they hired a registered nurse for their live-in nanny. When this nurse-nanny informed the Stone's that she was quitting, Iris's aunt recommended Iris for the job. Mrs. Richmond agreed, but she insisted that Iris have some experience with children first. Normally, it's difficult for an inexperienced nurse to secure a position in pediatrics. Being a famous actress, however, Lauren just made a phone call, and Iris was offered a position at Children's Hospital the very next day. In the meantime, she was invited to the Richmond's home to meet the girls.

Iris had been visiting the family two or three times a week since then. She'd always come home grinning like a monkey and stay that way for hours. I couldn't really blame her though. Like me, Iris grew up poor. For her, moving into that big mansion on the hill, even if only to join the household staff, was like a dream come true.

Friday was to be her last day at the hospital, then Iris was all set to start her new job. She was so excited she could barely contain herself. Why then, would she suddenly decide to take her own life?

She was the best friend I ever had, Doctor Simon. Hell, the only friend. I know I must accept the fact that she's dead. As hard as it is to comprehend, there's nothing in this world that can change that. What I can't understand is why she, of all people, would kill herself.

I am enclosing my phone number. I hesitate to bother you, doctor. But, if you have a moment, just hearing your deep, reassuring voice would give me comfort.

Respectfully,

Deirdre Garrison

Dr. Simon,

I awoke this morning convinced that Iris didn't kill herself. For one thing, where was the suicide note? When someone does something as desperate and irrevocable as killing themselves, they're usually trying to make a statement. Iris, in particular, was a very forthright person, not one to leave things unsaid. If she'd done this unspeakable thing, she would have left a note explaining why. And, what about her cocker spaniel, Baby? She adored that stupid dog, and she knew full well that I'm no animal lover. She would never have left him here with only me to care for him.

This can only mean one thing, of course. Iris was murdered!

With that in mind, I drove to the police station and asked to speak with the lead detective. You should see the police station, Dr. Simon. Bright and shiny with more windows than walls - it took me ten minutes to gather up enough courage to go inside. The secretary asked me to have a seat. A few minutes later, Detective Jacobs came out and introduced himself.

Jack, as he insisted I call him, is a scruffy looking character, but he has this way of making you feel at ease. He offered me coffee then led me to his office where we sat and talked for some thirty minutes or more. By the way, isn't that a funny name? "Jack Jacobs" Iris would've had a blast with that one.

I explained why I was certain that my friend hadn't committed suicide, and he seemed to take me seriously. Afterward, I was feeling pretty confident that the investigation was headed in the right direction. At least I *was* feeling confident. Then, I saw today's paper. There was Iris staring out at me from beneath the headline "Lauren Richmond's Nanny Takes Her Own Life."

My first thought was, where do they come up with this shit? She hadn't even started working for them yet! After thinking about it, I decided maybe it wasn't such a bad thing after all. At least the link to the Richmonds would draw attention to Iris's death making the police more inclined to investigate the matter further.

Another thought has occurred to me, Doctor. Where is the murderer now? Is it someone I know?

Sincerely,

Deirdre

Dear Dr. Simon,

    I phoned my supervisor today and took a leave of absence from work. I told her it's because I'm in a state of turmoil after the loss of my roommate. This is, of course, partly true. The main reason is that I intend on focusing all my time and energy into finding out exactly what happened to Iris.

    Since I wrote you last, I've been busy transforming the living room into a makeshift office. On one wall, I have a large map of the apartment drawn to scale, including the windows. I remembered that the deadbolt was locked when I got home from work that evening. Only Iris and I have keys, and hers were still in her handbag. This means that, even if she had unwittingly let the killer into the apartment, he would've had to leave through one of the windows. I'm also compiling a list of all of her friends, family members, and coworkers. I swear, that girl knew more people than I've met in my entire life.

    So far, I have two suspects. The first is Iris's ex-boyfriend Darren Saunders. Darren was crazy about Iris, but he was nothing more than a meal ticket to her. He used to take her to dinner, buy her clothes, loan her money, whatever she wanted. He even overlooked her cheating. Then one day, she decided that she didn't need him anymore and boom! Darren was history. Iris was a good friend to me, and she treated her patients with kindness. But, when it came to men, she just chewed them up and spit them out.

    My other suspect is our paperboy, James. The first time I met that little creep, I could tell there was something unsavory about him. When we moved in, he came around trying to sell us a subscription to the newspaper. We couldn't afford it, so Iris charmed him into giving us one for free. He never asked for money after that but kept bringing the paper every day like clockwork.

One day, when I came home early, I even caught him here inside our apartment. He made up some bullshit story about how he thought he heard Iris calling for help. She'd forgotten to the lock the door again, so it wasn't as if he actually broke in. I told Iris about it later and warned her to be more careful. She just laughed and said that James was harmless.

Iris and I were very different in that aspect. She was so open and trusting. I've always been suspicious of everyone.

Tomorrow is the funeral. They say that murderers often return to the scene of the crime. I'm hoping that they also attend their victim's funeral. The very thought of it makes me want to vomit, but I must control my emotions, for Iris's sake.

Yours truly,

Deirdre

Dear Dr. Simon,

They buried Iris today. The funeral home her parents chose had ample parking space, but there were still cars lined up around the block. Inside, the parlor was decorated with hundreds of fresh cut irises in every size and color. It was so crowded that I had to stand in line for fifteen minutes just to get to the casket. I had to do it though. I couldn't let my last memory of my beloved friend be the way she looked in that God-forsaken tub.

The mortician did an amazing job. She looked like an angel lying there… my Iris. Sleeping Beauty herself would've paled in comparison. All in white, her flaxen tresses were spread out like a fan across a lace-covered pillow. They had to dress her in long sleeves, of course, to cover those horrible gashes on her wrists. Seeing her again has convinced me more than ever that she couldn't have killed herself. That pretty face, so quick to smile, she loved life far too much to have even considered such a thing.

The viewing and funeral combined lasted four hours from start to finish, but the time seemed to fly by. I know it sounds crazy, but I found myself wishing it would go on forever. I guess, I knew once the services were done and they'd lowered Iris's body into the ground it would truly be over. It would all be over, and I'd have to go back to being plain old Deirdre, the girl nobody gave a damn about. I will never stop missing her, Doctor. *Never!*

I lagged behind at the funeral parlor after everyone else left for the cemetery taking snapshots of the guest book. I also managed to get a few discreet pictures during the graveside service. Utilizing an app on my phone, I sent away for 5x7 photographs. They should be here in a day or two.

Love,

Deirdre

Dr. Simon,

    I saw her, Dr. Simon! I swear to God, I saw Iris last night!

    I dreamt I was back in the funeral home, only this time there was no line in front of Iris's casket. The mourners were there, but the room was strangely quiet with no one making a sound. I peered at them curiously on my way to the casket, but I could not distinguish their features. It was like on television when they blur people's faces in order to protect their identity. The sight of them filled with me with dread, but as I turned away, I instantly forgot all about the other mourners. The casket had disappeared, and in its place stood our old clawfoot bathtub with Iris's pale, white arm draped over the side!

    That was the first thing I saw when I found her, before I even noticed all the blood. Terrified, I tried to turn and run away, but some unseen force pulled me forward. I wouldn't have thought it possible, but what I saw next frightened me even more. The body was coated with what appeared to be seaweed, and the face staring blindly upward was not Iris's. It was mine!

    I jerked up in bed, awakened by the sound of my own screams. The room was dark, so after catching my breath, I reached over and turned on the light. That's when I saw her. Iris was sitting on the foot of my bed smiling at me.

    What I don't know is *why* she came to visit me. Unfortunately, I didn't get a chance to ask. You see, Doctor, the light switch is not within easy reach, and as I was leaning out of bed when I saw her, the shock knocked me straight to the floor. I untangled myself from the sheets and sprang to my feet, but, by then, Iris was gone. But, I did see her, Dr. Simon. I swear it! She came back to tell me something, and I will not rest until I know what it is.

All my Love,

Deirdre

Dearest Doctor Simon,

    I got the pictures back today, and I now have another suspect. As I mentioned before, in the weeks leading up to her death, Iris was spending a lot of time with the Richmonds. So, their appearance at her funeral wasn't all that surprising. In fact, it was a little disturbing to me that, because of their presence, the whole thing was treated like some kind of media production. At least, the reporters and camera crews weren't allowed inside the funeral parlor or near the gravesite. I was just waiting for one of them to try it. They would have been sorry if they had!

    Anyway, taking snapshots of the guest book was easy, but it was a lot more challenging at the cemetery. Since some would have thought it inappropriate, I had to keep my phone hidden. I took as many pictures as I could, but many were of useless things such as grass or somebody's shoe. I did manage to get one decent, and in my opinion, very revealing shot of the actress and her husband. Lauren's classy, ageless face appeared void of emotion as she stood gazing down at the casket. It was the expression on her husband Xavier's face that caught me by surprise.

    I am, by no means, an expert at reading people's expressions, but the look of pure anguish captured in that hastily snapped photograph was unmistakable. Seeing it reminded me of something else that happened when Iris's aunt introduced me to the famous couple at the viewing. When Mr. Richmond took my hand, I caught a whiff of his cologne. It was a rugged, manly scent that I recognized immediately, but at the time I couldn't remember from where. Today, as I sat staring down at his handsome face in the photo, it came to me. It was in this apartment, Doctor! I have smelled that same exact fragrance right here in this apartment!

It was like the pieces of a puzzle started coming together in my mind. Iris never bothered much with her appearance. She was a natural beauty and didn't need to. Yet, every time she was planning to visit the Richmonds, she'd spend hours just getting ready. And, she was so excited about starting her new position. I mean, I know it was a great job and everything, but Iris practically glowed whenever she talked about it – especially when she mentioned *him*.

There were also those evenings when Iris said she was going out with someone. Then, after she left, that same person would call the apartment or stop by looking for her. It all makes sense now. The more I think about it, the more I'm convinced. Iris and Xavier Richmond were having an affair! How could she do that, Doctor? How could she?

Love always,

Deirdre

Dear Dr. Simon,

I hope, since none of my letters have come back, that you are indeed receiving them. I know you're busy, Doctor, but if you could drop me a quick note to let me know for sure, I'd be forever grateful.

Detective Jacobs "Jack" stopped by today. He seemed quite impressed with my efforts. I showed him the pictures I'd taken of the guest book, and he said it was very astute of me to think of it. Apparently, they already had copies of the guest book, but Jack asked if he could borrow the photos I took at the gravesite. I agreed, of course, but didn't mention the look on Xavier's face. I felt it best to let Jack draw his own conclusions. I didn't mention seeing Iris in my bedroom the night before either. I wanted to but was afraid he might think I was crazy.

I don't know what I'd do if I didn't have you to confide in, Doctor. If I had to hold this all inside I think I'd explode.

I should also probably tell you that Detective Jacobs is concerned for my safety. He said that from now on they'll be keeping a close eye on me. I don't mind telling you, I *am* a little scared. I've even started letting Baby sleep in my room. I've also hidden an extra-sharp butcher knife under my pillow.

Forever yours,

Deirdre

Dr. Simon,

This might be my last letter for a while. In fact, I'm not sure when I'll be able to post this one. As everyone else seems to have turned against me, I must tell you what happened the night before last.

It began with another nightmare. I dreamt I was trapped inside the casket with Iris's body, and I could hear someone shoveling dirt in on top of us. I tried to call out to let them know I was there, but when I opened my mouth nothing came out.

Then I heard another sound - a frenzied scratching noise. But instead of above, it was coming from somewhere down below. I awoke to find Baby scratching on the bedroom door. Thinking she needed to go out, I got up, flipped on the light, and started looking for my slippers. Before I could find them, Baby's whine had changed to a growl and she was clawing the woodwork so hard it left marks.

By then, I was good and scared, so I opened the door just wide enough for her to squeeze through and closed it behind her. In that brief instant that the door was ajar, a familiar scent wafted through the crack, and I thought I would die with fright.

Baby had no sooner left the room when she started barking like crazy. Seconds later, I heard a loud scuffling out in the living room. At first, it sounded like Baby was getting the better of someone. Then I heard a terrible wail, and I knew she'd lost the battle.

There's no lock on my bedroom door, and I had stupidly left my phone in the kitchen. I grabbed the knife from beneath my pillow and hid under the bed. Petrified, I stayed there, heart thrashing inside my chest.

After what seemed like hours, I thought perhaps the intruder had gone. Placing my hands on the floor in front of me, I started to pull myself out. That's when I heard it - footsteps right outside my bedroom door. Iris's murderer was coming. And, this time, he was coming for *me!*

I waited, eyes glued to the door, until morning, but no one ever entered the room. Just when I was about to doze off from sheer exhaustion, someone started banging on the front door and calling my name.

Jack! Thank God, it was Jack!

Relief poured over me. I scrambled out from under the bed and ran into the living room, where I found what remained of Baby. I know, I said didn't like the stupid thing, but after Iris died, that little dog was all I had left. I certainly wasn't prepared for what I saw. Baby had been mangled beyond recognition with blood and guts everywhere.

Jack was still banging on the door, so I made my way around the mess and flung it open.

Then the most peculiar thing happened, Doctor. When I opened the door, Jack and two other police officers just stood there, staring at me open-mouthed. I looked down and realized why. The knife was still in my hand, and both it and I were covered in thick, dark blood!

The Bainbridge Gazette April 1, 2017

ROOMMATE CHARGED WITH NANNY'S MURDER

Although the tragic death of Iris Anne Wilkes, a prior employee of Bainbridge Memorial Hospital and nanny for actress Lauren Richmond's two children, was previously deemed a suicide, new evidence has led to an arrest. Deirdre Marie Garrison, friend and former roommate of Wilkes, was taken into custody early yesterday morning.

Detective Jack Jacobs of Bainbridge PD states that when Miss Wilkes was found dead in their Baker St apartment, he immediately suspected foul play.

Garrison, also an employee of Bainbridge Memorial, was a prior suspect in the brutal murder of her psychiatrist, Dr. Andrew Simon, in 2015. But, that case remains unsolved. Another source tells us of a series of letters sent by Garrison to the doctor's previous address.

Garrison is being held for evaluation at Gentle Mercies Mental Health Facility.

CHAPTER 8

Unable to finish her sandwich, Peg listened in discomfort while Mac read the book aloud. What happened to the story about the swing? Or what about the one she read about the sea creature?

Finished, Mac shook his head, closed the book with a snap, and laid it on the counter. "Sounds like she was wacko. Hope she got the death penalty."

Peg frowned. Why didn't people get it? The whole point of the story was that in a mentally ill person's mind, the truth is often so warped and distorted that they can't be held accountable. That poor woman obviously didn't mean to hurt her friend. Peg stood up from the stool, grabbed her purse, and began looking for her wallet.

"You finished?" Mac nodded toward the half-eaten sandwich.

"Yes. It's delicious, but I need to get going. What do I owe you?"

"Don't worry about it," he said with a wave. "It's on the house."

"Really? Thanks!" Peg extracted a five from an inside pocket in her purse. "At least, let me give you a tip." She placed the bill on the counter and headed for the door.

"What about your book?" he asked.

"Keep it."

"Come on back now," Mac called as the door swung shut between them.

Once again, Peg skirted around the fresh asphalt then ran across the road to her car.

When she reached it, she stopped to peer in the backseat. She'd heard of murderers and rapists breaking into women's cars and hiding in the back, and she didn't want to become another statistic. It was empty, so Peg pulled out her keys and slid inside.

Lost in thought, she inserted her key and turned the ignition. Nothing happened. She tried again. Nothing. Even the barely perceptible whirring of the starter was absent. "Come on!" she screeched, smacking her hand against the steering wheel. The result was a painful throb in her wrist, but the car still wouldn't start.

"Fuck!" Peg got out of the car and stood fuming in the darkness. Then, feeling exposed and vulnerable, she got back inside. What was she going to do now?

Call for help. If this situation wasn't worthy of a 911 call, then that was just too damn bad. Grabbing her purse, she felt inside it for her phone. There was her wallet, her compact... Peg realized, with a sinking feeling in her gut, that her purse had felt a little lighter on her way back to the car. "No! No! *Nooo!*"

Peg jumped out and slammed the door. She must get back to the diner immediately. But, where was it? The bright glow she'd followed before was gone now. Squinting her eyes, she peered into the darkness. *There it is!* Peg let go of the breath she'd been holding when a sliver of light from an unknown source bounced off one of the diner's windows. The lack of light inside, however, meant that Mac was closing up. She had to stop him!

Running full force, Peg crossed the deserted street and dove straight across the asphalt, heedless to the damage to her shoes. Out of breath and frantic, she pummeled the door with both hands. "Mac? It's me, Peg! Let me in, Mac. *Please!*

She continued to pound on the glass until her knuckles were sore and the pain in her wrist had worsened. It was no use. Mac must've left right after she did. But how? Except for her car and the old van, there had been no other vehicles in sight. Lowering her arms, Peg fought back the tears. *Calm down,* she told herself as she turned and trudged back across the pavement.

When she reached the road, Peg stopped to look this way and that down the long lonely stretch of highway. To her left, she already knew there was nothing but abandoned factories. With a sigh of resignation, she turned right and started walking.

Up ahead, large barrier fences, the kind used to block noise from residential areas, lined both sides of the freeway. *Not much noise coming from this old road anymore.* Still, the existence of the fence could mean that there were houses lying somewhere behind them. Not that it mattered. Someone, a truck driver perhaps, was going to come along soon and give her a ride. But, did she really want to climb into a cab with a stranger? *It's not like you have lots of options.*

By the time Peg reached the towering metal barricades, not a single car had passed, and the seemingly never-ending road still stretched out before her. *This is unbelievable! There has to be some traffic through here.* She thought of the three women bikers. And, how could that diner have survived if this big four-lane road was no longer in use?

After several more minutes, Peg heard a vehicle approaching from behind. "Thank God!" she breathed, turning to face it. There was no time to lose as the car was all but flying, the driver evidently indifferent to speed limits.

Desperate to be seen, Peg waved her arms above her head. But the car showed no signs of slowing. In fact, it almost seemed to have sped up. When it passed beneath a streetlight, she observed that it wasn't a car after all but a pickup truck.

It was obvious that the truck had no intention of stopping, so Peg stepped back from the road nearly stumbling into the ditch behind her. As it whizzed past, she looked up to see three men wedged tightly inside the cab, their collective eyes glued to the road.

"Assholes!" Peg screamed as it drove away spewing exhaust fumes in her face.

Coughing, she brushed away the tiny bits of rubble that had landed on her skirt. What the hell was wrong with those people? They could've at least let her hop in the back.

The truck was barely out of sight when she heard another vehicle behind her. Peg turned to see not one, but two cars coming her way. "Must be rush hour." She attempted a laugh, but the result was more of a whimper. Determined to flag someone down this time, she hastened to the middle of the street.

The first automobile behaved exactly as the truck, accelerating as it passed with the lone driver refusing to look at her. Bewildered, Peg concentrated on the second, a large family car with at least two people inside. *This one's going to stop, damn it!* Clenching her teeth, she positioned herself directly in the vehicle's path. The car slowed then at the last minute, swerved to miss her. As it drove by, Peg attempted to make eye contact with the people inside, but just like the others, the man and woman pretended not to see her.

"What am I, fucking invisible here?" Peg shouted. As the car sped away, she discovered that someone, at least, had acknowledged her. A boy and girl twisted round in their seats were gawking at her through the rear window. Then their parents must've scolded them as they both dropped out of sight.

It was just a split-second glimpse, but Peg imagined she'd seen more than curiosity in those innocent little faces. She'd seen fear.

By now, her feet were starting to hurt and the alcohol she consumed earlier was giving her a headache. To make matters worse, there was a heavy feeling in the pit of her stomach. With one hand on her head, the other on her belly, she turned her attention to the barrier fence.

From where she stood in the middle of the street, Peg thought she could see a soft flavescent glow beyond the fence in the distance. *I'll bet that's a neighborhood.* In order to get past the fence however, she'd have to backtrack quite a ways. But wait! Up ahead to the right, a portion of the fence was agape. She began jogging toward it, but the jostling movement made her feel sick, so she slowed to a brisk walk instead.

When she reached the spot, Peg stopped and stared at the narrow fissure, like a gaping wound in the otherwise sound fencing. Directly in front of it, the guardrails were compromised with faded tire tracks leading off the road and into the fence. Apparently, someone lost control of their vehicle. Were there any fatalities? Pushing that thought from her mind, Peg peeked through the crack.

At first, there was only blackness. As her eyes adjusted, Peg realized that the moon provided stingy but adequate lighting to the landscape beyond. *This is insane. Maybe I should just go back and camp out in the car until morning.*

Trudging back to the road, Peg looked in the direction she'd come. Due to the distance and several burnt-out streetlights, the factories were no longer visible. How long had she been walking?

As she stood gazing down the timeworn highway, Peg was reminded of how very alone she was in the world. Her father disappeared when she was little, and her mother had succumbed to cancer last summer. Her brothers were too busy with their own families to pay Peg any mind, and now her lover was, no doubt, swaddled in the arms of someone new. What would happen if she didn't make it home alive? The only one who'd notice was Fred, and he probably wouldn't care until his food bowl was empty. Overcome with self-pity, Peg's throat clenched and her eyes grew moist.

Stop it! she checked herself. *You're going to leave this God-forsaken road and find a nice respectable looking house. Then, a quick call to the cops, and you'll be home safe and sound in no time.*

Peg whirled about and returned to the fence. After securing her purse around her neck, she attempted to squeeze through the jagged opening. She'd almost made it when a swift jerk told her that her purse was snagged. Cursing, she planted her feet and thrust her body forward. She burst through, lost her balance, and fell into the weeds on the other side. *Shit!*

Peg stood up, careful to maintain her balance on the uneven ground. The surrounding landscape was even darker than it appeared from the other side. Feeling a stinging sensation, she placed a hand on her outer thigh. It was warm and sticky. *Great! Now I'm bleeding.*

Closing her eyes, she took a deep breath. When she opened them, Peg found she could see a little better. The glow she'd glimpsed from the road was somewhere to the left of the opening, so zigzagging around the trees and skirt-catching bushes, she headed in that direction.

It didn't take long for Peg to realize that her chic little sandals, however fashionable, were not made for a late-night nature hike. The heels kept throwing her off balance, and the weeds scratched and tore at the exposed areas of skin on her feet and ankles.

Keeping the barrier fence to her left, she made her way, step by step, across the rugged terrain. Just when it seemed she was getting the hang of it, she came upon a six-foot high privacy fence. Having spent her youth running wild on a farm with two older brothers, Peg was undaunted. After examining the fence however, she discovered that it was smooth and slick with no place for a foothold.

Convinced that the key to her salvation lay just on the other side, Peg searched for a tree she could use to boost herself over the top. After determining that the closest ones were either too far from the fence or too small and spindly to support her, she continued down the fencerow.

Minutes later, she spotted the perfect tree. A young poplar had grown straight as an arrow right next to the fence. She slipped off her shoes, tossed them across, and climbed into it. But, Peg had forgotten about the sap, which sometimes oozes from that type of tree. By the time she made it to the other side, her hands were coated with a thick gluey substance. Even more discouraging, it appeared that the only thing on the opposite side of the fence was more trees and tangled undergrowth. Whispering obscenities, Peg pulled a tissue from her purse. She attempted to wipe the sap from her hands, but the paper stuck to her fingers and fell apart. She let it fall to the ground then, without thinking, reached up to brush her hair away from her face.

"Ouch!" Peg shouted, as, jerking her hand away, she liberated several long strands of hair from her scalp. "Son of a bitch!"

In response to her outburst, the insects in the surrounding weeds ceased their repetitive chirping. Peg had barely noticed the nocturnal sounds before, but now that they were absent, the resulting hush was so profound that it left her feeling like an unwelcome visitor in a crowded room. She lingered, quiet and still, until the insects resumed their nightly chorus then, recovering her shoes, she pressed on.

Some time later, Peg realized with a start that she'd lost sight of the barrier fence. It was then, the stupidity of her quest came raining down on her like a hailstorm. Was she going the right way? What if the glow she thought she saw earlier was nothing but wishful thinking?

All at once, the tears she had suppressed returned with a vengeance. This time, Peg let them flow freely, but silently, reluctant to disturb the nighttime harmony again. Swiping her face with the back of her hand, she peered up at the moon and then continued in what she hoped was the right direction.

After a time, she came to yet another fence. Smooth and slick as the first, it was perched atop a steep grassy knoll with no trees whatsoever close by. Clenching her fists, Peg let out an exasperated cry. "Why is this happening to me?"

As indignant rage pulsed through her veins, it alleviated the chill that had crept into her bones and left Peg with a strengthening feeling of resolve. She tried to hold onto it, but the anger faded as quickly as it had come leaving her feeling like a frightened child. She clambered up the embankment, turned her back to the fence, and allowed her body to slide to the ground. Pulling her purse across her stomach, she rested her arms across it and lowered her head. Beneath the purse's leather shell, she felt the edge of a flat rectangular object.

No, please. Not again. When she reached inside, the book felt cold and clammy. "Well, at least *you'll* never leave me," she muttered.

Overhead, the moon shone down like a giant desk lamp, so Peg pulled the book out, opened it, and began to read.

Yvonne T. Tibbs

CHAPTER 9
The Playmate

As I approached the shack, the chirping insects, the twittering birds, even the gentle rustling of the leaves ceased. Filled with an inexplicable sense of dread, I too stopped and stood waiting – for what, I didn't know.

I jumped when a massive crow split the stillness with a resounding caw. The bird, bigger even than Grandfather's rooster, flew down and landed with a soft thud on the edge of the broken-down porch. Emitting a putrid odor, like that of rotting fish, it cocked its head and appeared to be sizing me up. The freakish creature remained but a moment before flying away, carrying with it my last remaining speck of courage.

I'd had enough. Falling to my knees, I sobbed like a baby. Why, oh why did my parents send me to this God-forsaken place?

All at once, a mournful howl rang out from inside the shack. Vexation! He must've gotten trapped inside somehow. I got to my feet and stared at the derelict hovel. What was I to do? I couldn't just leave the poor dog there.

It was June 1953 and Father was sent home from the war with a shattered leg and sullen attitude. After several weeks of watching

Mother and I interact, he decided that I should spend my summer holidays with my grandparents in Northern Kentucky. Mother argued in my behalf, but Father had insisted. "He's eight years old and still acts like a baby. Spending time on the farm will help toughen him up."

He was mistaken. The wide, sprawling fields overwhelmed me, the cavernous barns with their foul-smelling stalls terrified me, and I could only view the animals from a distance.

I had always been a "Momma's boy." Born premature and small for my age, I never let Mother out of my sight. As she was inaccessible, however, Grandmother with her soft billowiness and flour-dusted apron made the perfect substitute.

"When ye gonna let go of yer Grandma's skirt-tail, boy?" Grandfather asked one afternoon. Grandfather was a hulk of a man with ruddy skin and darting green eyes. Hard of hearing, he shouted his words, spewing tobacco-stained spittle down his long bristly beard. I was afraid of him too. "Get on outside and play," he said. "She don't need ye underfoot."

"Jacob isn't bothering me," Grandmother said. "And, you know he's afraid to go outside by himself."

"Well, what in tarnation is he scared of?" Grandfather's voice echoed like thunder in the tiny, clean-swept kitchen. "Take Vexation," he told me. "He'll look after ye. Just make sure ye stay outta them woods!"

Vexation was Grandfather's prize coonhound and my only friend during that lonely summer. I obeyed of course, and minutes later the two of us were trouncing across a wide-open field. The sky was bright, the air was fresh, and my legs were like springs beneath me. Climbing fences and chasing squirrels, for the first time in my life, I felt giddy and carefree.

Time passed swiftly, and I was about to head home when I noticed a large, grass-covered knoll at the back of the field. Feeling curious and uncharacteristically brave, I called Vexation to me and together we ascended the hillock.

There it was - the dreaded woods, laid out before us like a vast, unfathomable sea. I nearly wet my breeches when a rabbit sprung out of the weeds by my feet, bounded down the hill, and vanished into the trees. Already in motion, Vexation emitted a long drawn-out cry like a police siren before diving in after it.

When the dog did not return, I ventured closer ready to take flight at the first sign of trouble. All along the perimeter, great hoary oaks huddled together as if plotting loathsome deeds. The narrow spaces between them put me in mind of certain alleyways back home – the ones which, when we passed, Mother would squeeze my hand and quicken her step.

I paced back and forth along the irregular but distinct line between sunlit field and darkened wood whistling and calling to no avail. Meanwhile, the shadows lengthened, my throat grew parched, and my stomach started to growl. I longed to go back but was afraid of what might happen if I returned without that infernal dog. Finally, fearing Grandfather's wrath, I entered the woods to look for Vexation.

The moment I stepped beneath the cool canopy of trees, I questioned my decision. The forest was like another world – somber, furtive, and unfriendly. No longer fragrant with honeysuckle and sweet annie, the air reeked of decaying wood, damp earth, and other odors I did not recognize. As I looked around, my empty stomach became secondary to a growing feeling of dread. What would happen if Grandfather found out I disobeyed him? More importantly, why had he warned me against the woods in the first place? Once again, I called for Vexation, but my voice sounded thin and girlish, so I continued the search in silence.

After a time, I acquired a *hunted* feeling. I imagined eyes peering out at me from the shadows and ears hearkening to my footsteps from behind the trees. Soon, every gnarled branch and clump of fungus looked exactly the same. It's no wonder that I became lost.

I was swiping hot tears from my cheeks when I stumbled across a stone path. Many of the stones were missing and others hard to find, but it seemed my only hope, so I began to follow it. Rounding a copse of saplings, I came upon a small clearing. It was like emerging from a long, lightless tunnel. I called for Vexation again, but there was still no response. I started to wonder if the dog had gotten past me somehow. Maybe he was already back in Grandmother's kitchen, slurping up yesterday's leftovers.

As I filled my lungs with the sweet, sun-warmed air, something on the other side of the clearing caught my eye. Hunkered behind a cluster of low-hanging trees, an old abandoned shack attempted to hide itself from the outside world. Gray and weathered, the squat, one-story building had a covered porch, which ran the length of its facade. Three narrow steps leading up to the porch had all but rotted away, and a jagged hole lay in wait by the door. Yet something about the dilapidated structure intrigued me, and I found myself moving toward it.

That's when the forest grew silent and a gigantic crow appeared.

After the bird flew away, I sank to the ground and was weeping when I suddenly heard a cry from Vexation. It seemed to be coming from inside the shack, so I stifled my tears and forced myself to ascend its narrow steps. From atop the porch, I could see a small pond just a short distance to the right of the shack. Surrounded by weeds, it wasn't visible from the clearing. There was nothing sinister about the algae-covered pool, yet, for some reason, the sight of it made me uneasy.

Averting my eyes, I approached the front door of the shack. The porch creaked and groaned with every step, and I cringed at the sound. Avoiding the hole, I reached out and tried the rusted latch. It refused to budge, so I turned my attention to a small dust-covered window.

All of a sudden, I noticed that the crow's horrible stench had returned. As my body tensed in response to the smell, I experienced an odd prickling sensation at the base of my skull. I scanned the area, but the bird was nowhere to be seen. Perhaps the offensive odor had a different origin. Ignoring it, I looked down at my feet testing the boards as I crept toward the window. Reaching it at last, I looked up, gulped a mouthful of fetid air, and grabbed hold of the sash for support.

A girl about my age was peering back at me from the opposite side of the glass. Her face was pale, her dress tattered, and her straw-colored hair appeared damp and uncombed. Despite all that, she was, by far, the prettiest thing I'd ever seen. Head low, her arms hung limp as tea towels at her sides. Full lips the color of roses were arched into a frown and her dark, soulful eyes glistened with tears.

The prickling sensation returned traveling further down my spine. The revolting smell, stronger now, brought bile to the back of my throat, and I could hear my own heartbeat pounding in my ears. It was as if my body sensed, even before I did, that the poor dejected waif was someone – *something* to fear.

"My name is Hannah," said a timorous voice. "Will you play with me?"

Although I heard the girl addressing me in clear dulcet tones, the window remained a closed barrier between us. Even more alarming was the fact that her lips hadn't moved.

Just then, Vexation commenced bellowing somewhere in the woods behind me. He wasn't in the shack after all. I swung my head around and when I looked back, the noxious smell hit me square in the face, stinging my eyes. I wiped them with my shirttail and peered into the window once more.

I was aghast! The girl was no longer visible as the inside of the glass was now suffused with a thick black substance. Horrified, I watched it eke out the outer edges of the windowpane, bubbling and popping like asphalt on a sweltering day.

"Will… you plaaaay with me?" The voice, no longer timid, sounded garbled and much deeper than before.

Before the scream could escape my lips, a powerful gust of vile-smelling air burst forth from the casement, knocking me backwards off the porch. Petrified, I curled into a ball on the ground and braced myself against the onslaught. As the toxic current swept over me, cold and biting as an ice storm, a long drawn-out wail accosted my ears. Wretched and terrible, it culminated into one high-pitched shriek then it and the icy blast were gone.

Too frightened to move, I remained in the fetal position for several minutes. When I finally popped my head up, I was shocked to see nothing had changed. The porch was empty, the dusty window still intact. Vexation howled again, and I realized that he was calling me. Drawing strength from his rich booming chords, I sprang up and ran not stopping until I was safe in my grandmother's arms.

Later that night, I awoke to the sound of weeping. My room was thick with that God-awful stench, and Hannah stood at the foot of my bed, radiant in the moonlight. Dark eyes shining, she renewed her appeal. "Will you play with me?"

I cowered beneath the bedclothes until morning.

The following night, I was not yet asleep when I detected the odor once more. Instead of weeping, this time the smell was accompanied by another noise. It sounded as if someone was dragging heavy sandbags across the floor. As I lay trembling beneath the bedclothes, praying for it to stop, something cold and hard clamped down on my leg. When my grandparents arrived in response to my screams, I had soiled the bed. My parents came to collect me the next day.

Years afterward, I begged off my summertime visits to the farm. When I was fifteen, my parents coerced me into returning by informing me that my cousin, Millie, would be there as well. One year older, with flaming red hair and a centerfold body, Millie could turn even a clergyman's head. It came as no surprise when she informed me that her mother had sent her to the farm in order to distance her from a certain *older* man.

At first, Millie seemed to be okay with the arrangement. Under her playful tutelage, I learned how to smoke cigarettes, steal cupfuls of Grandfather's hard cider, and curse like a sailor. After a while, however, she grew tired of me and opted to spend her time sulking in her room. I tried to draw her out, but next to Millie, I was as dull as dishwater with nothing to offer.

In desperation, I decided to share my harrowing experience from years earlier. By then, I'd convinced myself that the events of that time were just a product of nightmares and my eight-year-old imagination. Still, it made a rather good story. I began by telling Millie of a young girl living all alone in the woods.

"Whatever," she said. "Leave me alone, Jake."

"It's true," I persisted. "I've seen her."

Eyes wide, Millie latched onto my arm pressing me for details. I was quite pleased with myself until my cousin announced that she *too* wanted to meet Hannah.

"B… but, there's coyotes and snakes in those woods," I said, back-pedaling fast. "Maybe even bears! Besides, Grandfather won't allow it."

"If you're too *scared*, I'll just go by myself," Millie said with a flip of her hair.

The next day, the local church held evening services, which my grandparents never failed to attend. As Grandfather's truck sputtered down the driveway, Millie turned to me, her jaw set in determination. "I'm going to the woods to see if your story is true. You coming or not?"

After collecting flashlights, a pitchfork for Millie, and a hoe for me, we headed out across the fields. A rainstorm had passed through earlier that day leaving the ground damp and squishy. The trilling of insects in the grass around us was continually interrupted by Millie's loud curses whenever she stepped into a puddle.

Vexation tagged along, but as we drew near the forest, I noticed that the old dog's tail was tucked between his legs.

"Come on, boy," I said, stepping inside the tree line.

He looked up at me with cloudy eyes, whimpered, then turned and hobbled back to the house.

"Something's got Vexation spooked," I told Millie. "Maybe we should head back."

"Don't be silly. It's just a stupid dog."

We searched for what seemed like hours but couldn't find the path. "Please, Millie," I said. "It's getting dark. We really should head back."

She pretended not to hear me.

I saw no stones, but some time later, the woods grew eerily quiet as we stumbled into a clearing at the furthest end of which stood the old abandoned shack.

"There it is!" Millie cried, running toward it.

I followed her to the porch, but stayed on the ground as she clambered up the side. I reminded her of the hole by the door, but if Millie heard, she gave no indication.

"So, where's this crazy bitch you've been talking about?" she asked, looking around. "Hannah? Hannnnaaah."

I cringed as her cries seemed to echo off the trees. We waited, but the woods remained somber and still.

"I should've known you were full of shit!" Millie flung her pitchfork across the porch, barely missing my leg. "This entire family is full of shit!" Pacing back and forth, she hurled obscenities at the sky, the house, her mother for leaving her there, but mostly at me.

All at once, she stopped in her tracks pointing her flashlight directly in my eyes. "You hear that?"

"What?"

"It sounded like… a splash."

I thought about the little pond I'd seen last time, but I just shook my head.

"Hannah?" Millie sounded hoarse and unsure as she directed the flashlight beam to the window. "Hannah? Is that you?"

I thought Millie was pulling a prank. I *hoped* Millie was pulling a prank. But, when a prickling sensation commenced at the base of my skull and a familiar stench reached my nostrils, I realized the truth. I opened my mouth to warn my cousin, but all I could manage was a terrified squeak.

"What's wrong with you?' she asked, coming closer.

"P… please," I sputtered. "We have to go. *Now!*"

High above, the clouds parted as the moon peeped into the clearing illuminating Millie like an actress on stage. The look of indignation fell away from her face then, as if forgetting I was there, she turned and walked to the other side of the porch. When she reached the end, Millie halted and stood there, motionless and silent, as if waiting for something.

"Millie?"

Back rigid and arms at her sides, she didn't respond, but I noticed that her hands were shaking. All of a sudden, a low gurgling noise emanated from somewhere inside her throat and her body began to buck and sway to the rhythm of an unheard beat. Raising her arms to the sky, she whirled and gyrated, her long fingers curled inward like a raptor's claws clasping its prey.

Something warned me to stay quiet, but a gasp escaped my lips when Millie stopped dancing and crouched on all fours using the palms of her hands for feet. Squinting, she scanned the moonlit clearing. When she spotted me, her lips stretched back across her teeth in a sardonic grin. "*Now* will you play with me?" The voice was not Millie's.

A mind-numbing fear took me then, shaking my sense of logic and reason. But, there was one thing that I knew for certain. The creature known to me only as Hannah wasn't just the product of a nightmare or figment of my imagination. She was real! And, somehow some *way* she was inside Millie!

My heart faltered inside my chest. My body went flaccid with horror, and the flashlight and hoe fell to the ground. At that moment, the clouds drifted back over the moon. I dropped to the ground and fumbled in the darkness for my tools. Snatching them up, I aimed the flashlight at Millie just as she lunged across the porch, her pretty face contorted with rage.

"Why won't you *play with me?*" Scathing and shrill, her voice rent the air and shattered my senses. I tumbled backward just as Millie fell through the forgotten hole in the porch with a shriek.

Regaining my footing, I took a defensive stance, hoe in one hand, flashlight in the other. I hesitated a moment, paralyzed with fear and indecision, before persuading my reluctant legs to carry me to the edge of the porch. "Millie? You okay?"

She was lying face down with one leg wedged inside the hole. The other was curled around her body in an unnatural position – obviously broken.

"Millie?" I repeated.

She emitted a low shuddering sob before lifting her head to me. "Jake," she breathed, eyes wild with pain and confusion. "Help... me."

Before I could respond, a vulgar noise like someone slurping mayonnaise through a straw arose from the shadows to the right of the porch. I aimed my unsteady beam toward the sound.

My brain misfired and my breath caught in my throat when the circle of light flashed on the atrocity. I was standing face to face with a monster! The encounter lasted only a few seconds, but that terrifying image is permanently seared into my brain.

Whether upright or crouching, I couldn't say, but the beast towered over the two of us. With no neck, its ugly head protruded upward from its body like a huge malignant growth. Multiple horns, like that of a steer, erupted from its skull, and milky-white eyes peered out at me. Long elbow-less appendages hung limp at its sides, and what could've been wings, shot up from its back like two enormous scythes.

The disgusting noise I'd heard seemed to be coming from two long, mandible-like extremities that ran horizontally down its chin.

As Millie's screams filled the night, I closed my eyes and swung the hoe as hard as I could. With a sound like a large stone landing in a vat of fresh-churned butter, the sharp edge impaled the monster's forehead and stayed there, embedded in its tough leathery hide. The creature retreated with an ear-splitting squeal. Wrapping one of its muscular extremities round the handle, it snapped it in two before coming after me with long, earth-shaking strides.

I remember little after that. My feet flying beneath me while my body struggled to keep up. I never saw Millie again.

I awoke sometime later to the steady beeping of a hospital monitor. My grandmother later told me that I was discovered tearing down the road, wild-eyed and white as a sheet, with blood flowing from a gash in my forehead.

My grandfather, may he rest in peace, took to his bed and died shortly afterward. I never got the chance to ask him exactly why he forbade me to enter those woods. As for Millie, the authorities, with help from neighboring farmers, scoured the woods and surrounding areas, but neither my cousin nor the abandoned shack was ever found.

What roams that ancient forest in Northern Kentucky? To this day, I haven't a clue. But *that's* not the question, which haunts me.

Did Hannah, the hideous beast, the giant crow, the friendless little girl, finally acquire a playmate?

CHAPTER 10

Peg stood up and flung the book as hard as she could into the shadows. Readjusting her purse, she descended the grade and began walking alongside the fence searching for something, anything, she could use for a foothold.

After venturing further down the line, Peg found what she needed. It looked as if part the fence had been damaged at some point and a new section added. Instead of attaching it properly however, someone had simply nailed the section in place with two-by-fours.

By the time Peg finished scaling the second fence, she'd added several splinters and a scraped knee to her injuries. She paid them no mind however, when she saw what lay spread out before her. Acre upon acre of blessedly short, meticulously manicured, grass! *Thank God!*

Spirits soaring, Peg bounded downhill across the gently sloping yard in search of the house that went with it. Her renewed energy lasted only briefly however, giving out when she came to a close-knit stand of pines. Was this just some kind of park or golf course?

As she stood in silent speculation, it seemed as if every part of her body throbbed, ached, or just plain hurt. And, she was tired - so very tired. The ground beneath the trees was coated with moss and a layer of pine needles. With a small defeated sigh, Peg lowered herself onto it. For a moment, it felt like heaven; then the needles scratched and bit, and a deep, numbing coldness rose up from the ground. With no more ideas and no place left to go, she curled into a fetal position and wept.

Protruding up from the ground beneath her, a rock pressed painfully against Peg's thigh. As she changed position, a faraway flicker of light caught her eye. Placing both hands on the ground, she swallowed her tears and attempted to find it again.

There, in the distance, was the unmistakable glow of civilization. Afraid to let the tiny beacon out of her sight, Peg began crawling toward it. More than once, her hair got entangled and her knees scraped roots jutting up from the ground, yet she kept going.

When at last she emerged, Peg met with yet another obstacle in the form of a steep incline leading down to a pond. Instead of despair however, she was filled with relief when she saw what lay further beyond. It was neither a suburban plat nor a crowded neighborhood but a single grandiose mansion in the centermost part of a secluded valley.

There you go, she told herself, *a nice respectable looking house.* But an unusually shaped one she noticed. Instead of having towers, gables, or other florid architecture one might expect from such an imposing dwelling, the three-story building was square, like a colossal box with a roof on top.

Peg also noted that the dark foreboding house was not the origin of the light she had followed. The glow she spotted from the road, then again from beneath the trees, came from numerous lampposts that encircled the house and lined a long winding driveway, the end of which ran out of sight.

But, what set the home apart from anything Peg had ever seen were the far-reaching gardens that surrounded the house. From her elevated point, she observed a labyrinth of paths meandering through trees, shrubs, and all manner of plants, none of which she could identify from so far away. There were also fountains, gazebos, and, what looked like, huge topiaries.

Taking a deep breath, Peg rose to her feet despite objections from every muscle in her body. "Just a little bit farther," she muttered.

After lowering herself over the edge, she carefully began her descent. Halfway down, a narrow projection of earth beneath her feet gave way and she fell some five feet or more to the bottom. No longer caring about her appearance and benumbed to the pain, she got back up and dusted herself off.

Detecting a foul odor, Peg then turned her attention to the body of water directly in front of her. As she leaned over it, the smell that accosted her nostrils was so disgusting, she could feel bile and the remains of her loose-meat sandwich rise up in her throat. She jerked back, clapping a hand over her nose and mouth. *What in the world?*

And, something else was off about the pond. What was it? Holding her breath, she leaned over the fetid pool once more. There was no reflection! Although the sky was cloudless and the moon and stars glistened brightly overhead, Peg could see nothing in the dark stagnant water. Averting her eyes, she stood and made her way to one of the pathways she hoped would lead to the house. As she walked away, a barely audible splash made her stop and look back. Was that a ripple in the pond? No. Nothing could possibly survive in that nasty water. Whirling about, she hastened down the path.

The strategically placed lampposts illuminated her surroundings, but the shadows they cast were long and unnerving. Now, close enough to touch them, Peg found that she was still unfamiliar with much of the plant life. Vivid, in unnatural shades of orange, pink, and green, instead of growing straight and tall, they clustered together with no sign of flowers or fruit. They didn't even, she realized with a start, have branches. The topiaries were equally unusual. Living depictions of imagined monsters, they reminded her of pictures she'd seen of deep-sea creatures with gaping mouths and bulging eyes.

As she continued toward the house, eyes darting this way and that, Peg realized that her newfound haven was farther away than it had appeared. She stopped for a moments to catch her breath. Her feet throbbed, her back ached, and it was an effort just to keep her eyes open.

At last, she stood just a few yards away. Even bigger up close, the outer walls of the mansion seemed to stretch upward and outward forever, making her feel small and insignificant. As her eyes swept over the extraordinary abode trying to take it all in, she couldn't help but think something was missing. Then it hit her. There were no windows, at least not as far as she could see. *Weird!*

Despite the fact that Divinity and its surrounding areas were replete with backwoods lore and superstition, Peg had never been one to indulge in fantasies. From the moment she stepped onto the property, however, she'd been battling a growing sense of foreboding. It was at its strongest now making her hands shake and her stomach churn. Peg looked back across the garden in the direction she had come. It wasn't too late. She could still turn back. *Stop being ridiculous*, she told herself as she turned and walked to the front of the house.

Rounding the corner, she observed a huge cascading fountain. While fighting her way through the unforgiving landscape, Peg hadn't really thought about her appearance. As she contemplated knocking on a stranger's door in the middle of the night, she realized how she must look – hair in disarray, dried blood on her leg, and mascara, no doubt, streaming down her cheeks. Perhaps she could use the water from the fountain to freshen up a bit. Veering from the path, she stumbled toward it.

The frothy water looked clear and inviting, but when her eyes strayed to the alabaster statues at the center of the fountain, she abruptly came to a halt. All of them nude, they appeared to be life-size depictions of young men and women. Although not one to be easily offended, Peg considered their obscene poses and facial expressions both shocking and distasteful. Equally disturbing were their gross physical deformities ranging from webbed fingers and toes, to large misshapen claws and feelers where arms, legs, and other appendages should be.

"I guess that's what you call modern art," she muttered.

Before dipping her hands in the water, she retrieved the compact with mirror from her purse and peeked inside it. It was worse than she feared. Hair wild and cheeks streaked with mascara, she looked like some kind of spaced-out rock star. Placing her compact on the edge of the fountain, she rummaged for a tissue. Finding none, she untucked her blouse, moistened the hem in the fountain, and, leaning forward in an awkward position, used it dab her face.

As she stood by the constantly flowing water attempting to make herself presentable, Peg was overcome by a pressing need to urinate. She sized up a nearby bush, but the yard was well lit and she suspected there could be hidden security cameras hidden amongst the foliage. Doing her best to suppress the urge, she grabbed her compact to reassess the damage. No longer frightful, now she just looked pale and weary. It would have to do.

Yvonne T. Tibbs

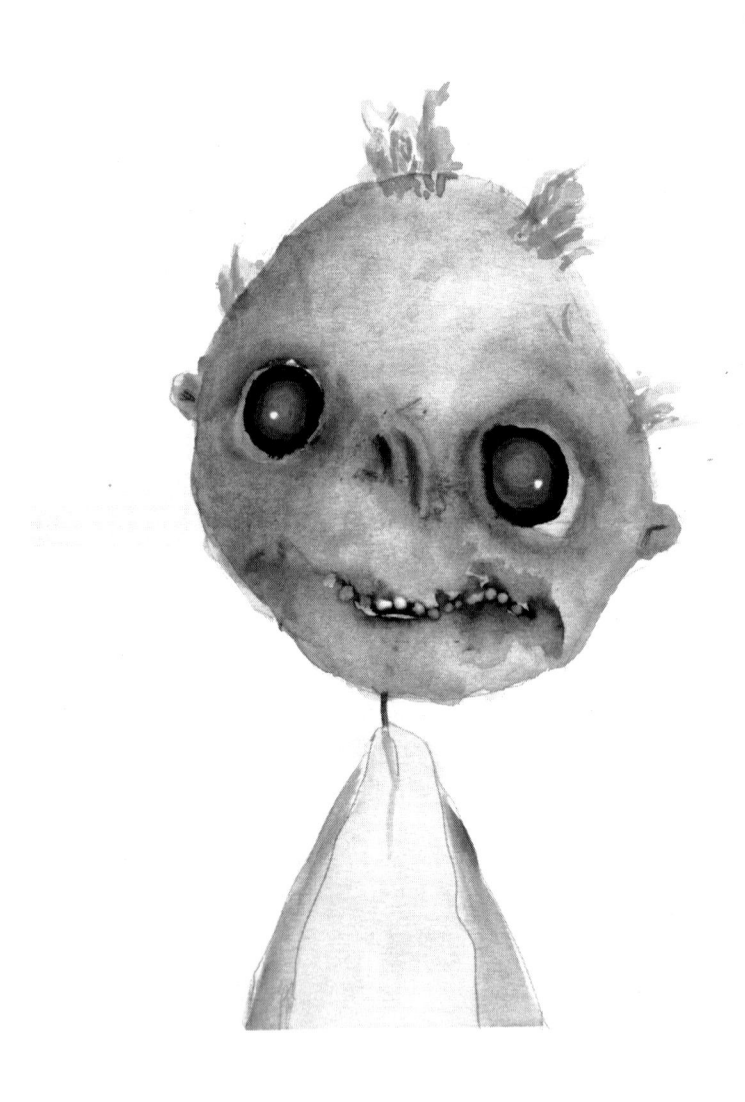

CHAPTER 11

Peg took one last look at the statues centering the fountain. What kind of people would own such a thing? She shuddered as she turned and headed for the house.

Moments later, she ascended the steps to a small, unremarkable front porch. Before her stood a large metal door with only a tiny peephole for adornment. She eyed the buzzer to the right of the door but decided to try knocking first as it stood less chance of waking the entire household. At first there was no response, but just as she reached for the buzzer, the door began to open slowly inward.

Having expected someone taller, Peg was obliged to take a step back and lower her gaze when a child of around seven or eight emerged. She had been rehearsing what to say, but the words got lodged in her throat when the boy's features came into view. Possessing a pale, somewhat grayish pallor, the skin of the child's face and hands was stretched to near-translucency with a smattering of dark blue veins just beneath the surface. Sparse, straw-colored hair grew in patches across his scalp, and lieu of a nose, two elongated nostrils ran down the center of his face. His abnormally wide mouth curved downward in a seemingly permanent frown, and his lips were non-existent.

It was his eyes, however, which had rendered Peg speechless. Wide and glistening, they were a metallic color one would not normally associate with eyes. Bronze she decided, like her favorite pair of earrings, with unusually large pupils. The porch light seemed to bother the boy, she noticed, when he blinked and stepped back into the darkened entryway.

As she struggled to find her voice, Peg was reminded of the horribly disfigured children she encountered when her nursing class toured a pediatric burn unit. This poor waif must have suffered a similar accident.

"Hello," she began. "My name's Peg. What's yours?"

She couldn't see him as well now, but it looked as if the boy's face was void of expression. As the silence grew louder between them, Peg wondered if he was able to speak.

"My name is Numo," he said at last.

Once again, Peg was struck speechless. From out of that grotesquely formed mouth, a melodious choirboy voice had emerged.

"Well… Numo, I'm sorry to disturb you. Bu… but I've had some car trouble, and I was hoping to use your phone." *Calm down, you idiot!*

Instead of answering, the boy continued to stand, one hand on the doorknob, and look her over. As his remarkable orbs traveled with erratic, jerking movements from her unruly hair to her scuffed and dirty shoes, Peg found herself feeling foolish and even a little… what was it? Intimidated! She felt intimidated!

This is ridiculous! He's just a little boy. "Can you please let someone know I'm here," she said, trying to hide the irritation from her voice.

"You may come in." Numo pushed the door open further, turned, and walked back inside.

As she entered the dimly lit vestibule, Peg was unsettled by a noticeable drop in temperature. The air outside had been cool, but bearable. Now it felt as if she was walking into an operating room, frigid and sterile.

Seconds later, they emerged in a grand foyer, the likes of which Peg had never seen. An enormous semi-circle, it rose some thirty feet or more with a majestic two-sided staircase at the far end. A large chandelier dangled above it with similar but smaller ones arranged in perfect symmetry along the outer edges of the room. Although elegantly wrought, the peculiarly shaped fixtures did little to illuminate the expansive chamber.

The main source of light, it seemed, was coming from massive fish tanks imbedded in the black granite walls. Eight in all, they stretched from floor to lofty ceiling on both sides of the room. Large gilded mirrors rested on the wall-space between each of the aquariums for a stunning but somewhat overwhelming effect.

"Wait here," Numo instructed. Abandoning her, he proceeded to one side of the staircase.

As Peg watched his slight figure move slowly and methodically up the long flight of steps, she noticed for the first time that he was wearing pajamas embellished with tiny moons and stars. He was such an odd little thing. There was something almost… *inhuman* about him.

When he was out of sight, Peg crept closer to one of the mirrors. "God, you look hideous!" she whispered.

After plucking the last of the pine needles from her hair, she stepped back to admire one of the fish tanks. Her eyes were immediately drawn to a school of silver fish that shot past the glass like tiny underwater missiles before disappearing behind the wall to the right of the mirror. A split-second later, Peg caught a glimpse of the same flash of silver in the aquarium on the left side of the mirror. *What the…?* Puzzled, she walked out to the center of the room to better see the entire wall.

Only then, did it register that what she thought were individual aquariums were in fact apertures into the giant aquatic world now surrounding her. The knowledge left Peg with the unsettling feeling that she, herself, was the one on display.

A burst of neon blue lured her attention back to the same spot where she observed a second school of fish scattering in all directions. Peg clapped both hands over her mouth to stifle a scream when the reason for their frenzied behavior emerged from somewhere below. Dark and shimmering, with an enormous head and eel-like body, the man-sized creature fit the description of the deep-sea monster she read about in that god-forsaken book. With barbed protrusions across its back and a mouthful of dagger-like teeth in its gaping jaws, it was exactly as Peg had pictured it. Before she could reflect on this extraordinary revelation, however, her amazement turned to fear when the animal came to a stop and looked directly at her.

It can see me. Oh God! He can see me.

As the gruesome beast drifted closer to the glass, Peg reminded herself that, whatever it was, it could not escape its watery prison. Yet, she couldn't stop her heart from racing when she met the creature's gaze.

After a time, Peg realized that she was no longer focused on the animal's cold unfeeling eyes, but on a long, skinny spike jutting out from his chin. To her astonishment, the tip of the spike lit up with an unnatural glow and began to wiggle back and forth. Then, without warning, the brute turned his big ugly head and, with a flip of his tail, was gone.

Dizzy and light-headed, Peg was dismayed to discover that she was now standing mere inches from the glass!

"He was trying to hypnotize you," Numo said.

Startled, Peg turned to see that the boy had noiselessly returned. "Well he was doing a good job," she said. "What *was* that anyway?"

Numo shrugged. "Just a fish. Mother said she will be down shortly."

Until that moment, Peg had assumed that the boy was going to fetch a butler or housemaid to assist her. Surely, a home this size had some sort of staff. "Oh dear. I hope you didn't get her out of bed."

"It's okay. We keep late hours here. Besides, she'll be glad to see you." Although Numo's mask-like face displayed no emotion, his eyes burned with an almost predatory gleam.

You're just imagining things, Peg told herself. Meanwhile, a sharp twinge in her abdomen signaled that her bladder was stretched to its limit.

"I'm sorry, Numo, but could you please show me to a bathroom? I'll only be a minute."

Before he could respond, the room grew brighter with a green luminescence just as a lusty voice floated down from above.

"Well now, if it isn't the party girl."

Peg turned to greet her hostess, but the words congealed on her tongue. Standing atop the picturesque staircase, arms stretched languidly across the bannister, was Macushla Whitman!

Oh fuck!

Now, in the privacy of her own home, Macushla had assumed a much different appearance. Her jet-black tresses, no longer restrained, tumbled in waves about her shoulders, and the ill-fashioned dress from the party had been replaced with a beautiful gown. Bedecked with what appeared to be hundreds of emerald rhinestones, the form-fitting smock appeared to be the origin of the light, projecting a viridian haze as it reflected off the numerous chandeliers.

Muscles taut, Peg tried to smile as she forced her unwilling legs to carry her to the bottom of the stair. As she drew closer, she couldn't help but notice how very different the woman looked. Beneath her stunning gown, Macushla's ample breasts sat high and firm. Her upper body, normally cloaked with a tent-shaped dress, was both lean yet curvaceous. And, despite the distance, Peg could see that her eyes sparkled, as if lit from inside. As she stood, swathed in the pale green aura, Macushla's beauty was nothing short of breathtaking.

It was then, Peg realized that, not only had she failed to address her hostess, but she was gawking up at her like a fool. Swallowing hard, Peg was still thinking of what to say when Macushla glided out from behind the balustrade. Words failed her after that.

The monster, as monster it was, only resembled a woman from the waist up. It was now staggeringly obvious that there was *no* form-fitting gown. Macushla Whitman lovely and radiant was naked as a newborn babe. What had appeared to be some type of silky material was, in reality, flesh - the rhinestones, her resplendent emerald scales.

Yet, most dreadful of all was the lower half of her anatomy. It was no mystery as to why Macushla had chosen to shed her cumbersome clothing in the privacy of her own home. How difficult it must've been to corral all those long slender tentacles underneath her skirt. Extending from just below her umbilicus all the way to the floor, they obviously served as legs, but, unlike human appendages, each serpentine member seemed to have a life of its own. Dark and sinewy, they too glistened as she descended the stairs.

At first, Peg heard nothing but the sound of her own heart thrashing in her chest as Macushla slithered silently toward her. Then, out of nothing, a soft humming, a *familiar* humming, arose. As it flowed through her body, like water through a sieve, Peg became aware of a sinister force tugging at her consciousness. Clueless as to how to fight it, she could actually feel her memories being erased and her will shattered. She couldn't remember where she was or how she had come to be there. And, as the warm wet urine trickled down her inner thighs, Peg suddenly forgot how to breathe.

CHAPTER 12

Peg awoke inside a luxurious bedchamber. Her head was pounding and her mouth was parched, but the bedclothes swaddled snugly round her body were soft and warm. *Where am I?*

As she pulled herself to a seated position, the velvety coverlet fell away revealing her naked breasts. "Oh, my God!"

Grasping the top sheet, Peg covered herself and looked around. The king-size bed she lie on had four fluted bedposts, like silent wooden sentries on each corner. The tasseled canopy overhead, as well as the bedding, carpet, and wallpaper were varying shades of lavender. Being Peg's favorite, she had the fleeting thought that the room could've been quite lovely if not for the notable lack of furnishings. Other than the bed, the only other thing in the room was a small three-legged table. Her clothes were nowhere to be seen.

What the hell had happened? Peg tried to remember, but her thoughts were muddled and her head felt like a bowling ball sitting atop her shoulders. *You're probably just hung over,* she told herself. Wasn't she on her way to a party last night?

It was then, Peg noticed that there were two doors leading from the room. The one directly across from the bed was obviously an exit, so the other must be - a bathroom?

Water! What she needed most right now was some water.

Moving slowly, Peg wound the sheet round her middle and stumbled out of bed. The bathroom proved to be utilitarian with a bathtub, toilet, and sink. Peg turned on the faucet, then, spotting a glass on the counter, held it under the nozzle. As she guzzled, Peg recalled filling something else with water… a bowl, yes that was it, and giving it to Fred. Poor Fred. Did he have enough cat food to last until she got home? Home – the little one bedroom apartment she rented when she got her new job.

All at once, the floodgates burst with events from the previous night flashing by so fast it made Peg dizzy, the boring drive through the countryside, the crowd of strangers laughing, drinking, *leering*. Sasha handed her a glass and then… As the succeeding events made themselves known, Peg loosed her grip on the counter and slid down onto the cold tile floor.

No. That couldn't be right.

Gathering herself up on unsteady legs, she lurched from the room and to the outer door. It was locked. "Let me out!" Pounding the door with one hand, Peg held the slippery sheet in place with the other. When no one responded, she returned to the bed where she sat, head in hands, trying to quell the panic that was rising in her chest.

After several minutes, something occurred to her. Was she still at the party? Of course! She'd spent the entire evening drinking alcohol on an empty stomach and it had simply proven too much for her. Someone, Sasha probably, must've led her to this room to sleep it off. Breathing easier, Peg lie back on the bed and gazed up at the canopy. What a crazy dream!

But… why had they taken her clothes? And, why did they lock the door?

A faint clicking sound was followed by the sound of a door opening inward. Peg held her breath as she rose up on her elbows to see who it was.

Although wrenched from her own throat, Peg's scream seemed to emanate from every corner of the room as it bounced off the walls and reverberated in her ears. It was true – the windowless house, the monster behind the glass, Macushla with her long… Peg's body felt light and weightless as unconsciousness threatened to return.

Across the room, Numo slipped inside and shut the door behind him. "Shhh!" He whispered, an emaciated finger poised where his lips should be. "They'll hear you."

Peg pulled the bedclothes up to her neck, her body shaking uncontrollably. "Wha…" she stammered. "What do you want?"

"Calm down," Numo crooned. Still in his pajamas, as the boy approached the bed, Peg saw that he was clutching something to his chest. "I was hoping we could be friends," he said. "Look, I even brought some of your clothes."

As Numo held out the bundle he was been carrying, Peg recognized her ruffled blouse and little black skirt. She closed her eyes for a moment, attempting to free herself from the hysteria that held her. *Just play along, Peg. Just play along.* "Oh, th… thank you."

Keeping a firm grip on the sheet, she held out her other hand. As she accepted the clothes from Numo's outstretched arms, the tip of her fingers brushed his skin. It felt cold and clammy like a fish pulled straight from the water. She cringed inwardly while trying to smile, then, using the coverlet as a shield, she yanked the blouse over her head and slipped into the skirt.

"I get so lonely sometimes," Numo said. "Rosa used to read to me, but she's gone now."

"Rosa?" Peg thought of the missing women she'd read about.

"She was pretty… Like you." Then, for the first time, Numo smiled at her. As his paper-thin lips drew taut across his vile little face, they exposed not human teeth, but jagged saw-like edges atop pallid gums.

As her peripheral vision narrowed, Peg could see nothing but those razor sharp points. Feeling her consciousness waning again, she wrenched her gaze from his face. To hell with playing along! She had to get the fuck out of this crazy place! Using her fear as a catalyst, she leapt from the bed, flung the sheet over Numo's head, and gave him a shove. Three long strides and she was standing before the door. Peg grabbed the knob and twisted, only to find that it was locked again.

"That wasn't very nice."

When she turned to see Numo emerge from beneath the sheet, Peg felt as if she were seeing him for the very first time. This was no accident victim. Like Macushla, he too was a monster!

But, he was only a little monster. And he had the key. Should she try and wrest it from him? Peg thought of Numo's jagged teeth. "I'm sorry," she said. It's just… I'm a little frightened."

"Yes." He sighed. "They always are."

Peg's struggled to maintain her balance. *They?*

"But, I won't hurt you," Numo added. "Not if you promise to be my friend."

"I… I think I'd like that, Numo."

His eyes glistened, and Peg feared he would flash his dreadful smile again. "Then you must read to me," he said. "Rosa always read to me."

"B… but, we don't have anything to read." Peg tried to think. "Is there a library here? Or, maybe you have some books in your room?"

"What about that one?"

Peg turned to where Numo was pointing. Centered atop the three-legged table was that damnable little book.

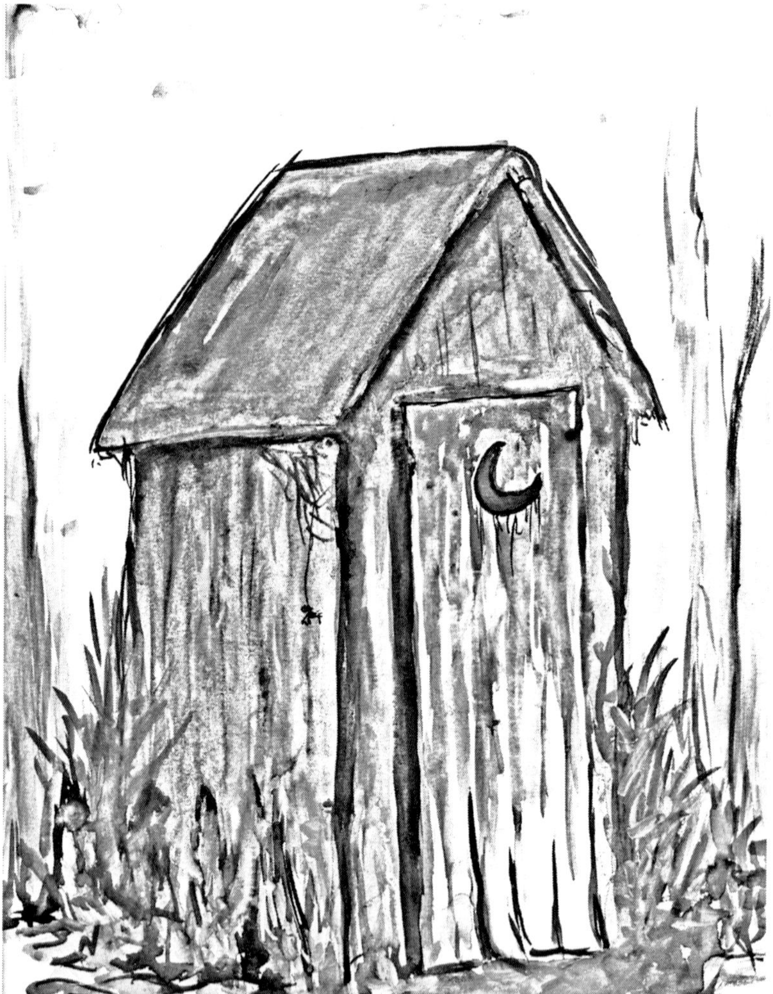

CHAPTER 13

The Crescent Moon

I don't mind sitting in back. Somebody has to. *Right?* It's just that I get a little carsick sometimes. If I concentrate and keep my eyes forward, I should be okay. If I'd been thinking ahead, I could've snitched some of Mom's Dramamine. I never think ahead.

"Ain't that right, Dabney?"

"Huh?" I didn't hear what they said, and now Paige and Chloe are laughing at me.

"Never mind," Chloe says. "Hey, stop here," she tells Paige. "We need papers."

Paige pulls into the little Stop-N-Rob just outside of town. This is great! Chloe and Paige, two of the prettiest, most popular girls in school, invited me, dull Dabney Taylor, to go to the lake with them. God, I hope somebody sees us. I'm going to play it *so* cool.

We get out and my head is spinning. It's probably just nerves or the fact that I haven't eaten – and the carsickness of course.

Paige tells Chloe that her ass is hanging out the bottom of her shorts. Chloe sticks out her tongue and pulls them up even higher. She keeps them that way and we walk inside. I don't know why she does stuff like that. I'd say it was to get attention, but with those boobs and that thick blonde hair, Chloe gets all the attention she wants.

The little bell rings above our heads; then Paige and Chloe head for the beer cave. What are they doing? They know we're not old enough to buy beer. I feel like an idiot just standing there, so I follow them into the icy room.

When I get there, Chloe is running her fingers across the wine coolers. "What's your pleasure, Dabney?" she asks me.

"The wild berry looks good," I say, trying to keep my teeth from chattering.

"Wild berry it is." She grabs a four-pack.

Paige snags some beer; then we hit the snack aisle.

The little bell rings again, and a stocky guy with dark curly hair walks in. He's wearing a shabby red and black flannel jacket over a dirty white t-shirt. Just looking at him makes me feel sweaty. Not exactly appropriate for Ohio in August.

"Good evenin'," he says.

I smile, but Paige and Chloe just ignore him. As he walks by, I catch a whiff of cigarettes and body odor.

I grab a bag of Fritos and Chloe gets some M&Ms. Paige shoves a Milky Way down her pants, and I pretend not to notice.

When it's our turn at the register, they set their beer and stuff on the counter. Paige grabs my Fritos and throws them down too.

"We need a pack of one-point-five's," Chloe tells the guy behind the counter.

"You girls rolling your own cigarettes?" He grins. He's kind of cute, but he's like twenty-something. "I'll need to see some ID." He nods toward the alcohol.

"How's this?" Chloe steps away from the counter and raises her top. Her nipples are dark brown and huge. I can't help but stare.

"What the fuck are you looking at?" she asks.

At first, I think she's talking to me, and I can feel my face getting hot. Then I smell something gross, and I realize that the curly-haired guy is right behind me. He's staring at Chloe too, and he's got this weird look on his face. It almost reminds me of… *hunger*.

The guy behind the counter laughs. "Looks good from here. Where you ladies headed?"

"The lake," Paige says. "Wanna come?"

"I wish. I'm stuck here until midnight."

"Poor baby." Chloe purses her lips.

She and Paige head back to the car, but I stay behind and buy a one-time dose of Dramamine from behind the counter. I pop them in my mouth and swallow them dry.

On my way back to the car, I notice some dark clouds in the distance. "Oh please don't let it rain," I whisper. I don't want anything to spoil this day.

I slide back in the car, and Chloe hands me a wine cooler. I try to open it, but the little ridges hurt my palm.

Chloe rolls her eyes and gives me her open one.

"Where's the smoke?" Paige asks me.

I dig in my pocket for the little baggie of pot. It's the first time I've actually bought my own, and it makes me feel important and nervous at the same time. I hand it to Paige as if passing on the Olympic torch, and she starts rolling a joint.

"Gimme a beer," she tells Chloe.

Paige's hands are full, so Chloe holds the bottle while she drinks. A little dribbles onto her shirt and we all laugh.

"What does that old fucker want?" Chloe sits up straighter in her seat.

I look out, and the curly-haired man is staring at us as he walks past our car. I wouldn't exactly call him old. He's probably in his thirties, I guess. I gasp when he comes to a stop.

"You know what he wants," Paige says.

"Gross!" Chloe pretends to gag.

I fake a laugh while I study the man's face. He doesn't notice because he hasn't taken his eyes off Chloe. He's frowning and clenching his fists. I wish she hadn't been so mean to him. I watch as he gets into a red pickup truck and drives away. *Whew!*

Paige lights the joint and passes it to Chloe. I love the way pot makes me feel, but I hate the smell. It reminds me of when Grandma used to pick weeds from her yard, boil em on the stove, and call it food. *Yuck!*

The car moves, and I feel like puking again.

Chloe takes a hit then leans over the seat to pass it to me. "You okay? You look a little green. Doesn't Dabney look a little green?" she asks Paige.

Paige looks at me through the rearview and grins. "Ribbit!" she says. She starts laughing and chokes on the smoke she was holding in. The car veers off the road. Paige jerks it back, and Chloe's head whacks the passenger side window. I fall to the side too, but I manage to hold onto the joint and my drink.

"Hey! Watch it, bitch!" Chloe says, rubbing her head.

"Sorry," Paige says, but she's still grinning.

Chloe frowns at Paige then looks back at me. "That'll make you feel better," she says when I hit the joint.

I cough and nod.

After a while, the motion sickness is better, but the pot is making everything seem bigger somehow. I don't remember it making me feel like this before. I take a drink of my cooler and look around. There's a red pickup truck right behind us. *Oh no!* I choke on my drink.

"You ok back there?" Chloe asks me.

I swallow hard and lean my head over the seat. "I think that guy from the Stop-N-Rob is behind us."

"What the hell is a Stop-N-Rob?" Paige asks.

"You know, the convenience store."

Chloe leans over the seat. Paige looks in the rearview.

"It *is* him," Chloe says. "That son of a bitch is right on our bumper."

"You guys are fucked," Paige says. "That's not him."

"No seriously," I say. "I recognize the truck." I'm talking fast now and sitting on the edge of my seat.

"Ignore him," Paige says.

I face forward, but I can still see the truck in the rearview mirror. He's getting closer. I can't take it anymore. I turn back around and see him scowling down at us, both hands on the steering wheel. Now, all I see is his grill. If he doesn't slow down he's going to - I cringe and duck my head.

"*Thunk!*"

Chloe screams.

"He hit us!" Paige yells. "That fucker actually hit us!"

A man and woman in a dark gray sedan pass us on the other side of the road, and the truck slows down. We start to pull away, and I can see the man's face clearly now. He is staring straight at me and he's - he's *grinning*.

"We gotta call the cops!" I say.

"Yeah right, dumb-ass." Paige holds the joint up to the mirror. "Can you believe her?" she asks Chloe.

Chloe doesn't answer. She's peeping over the back of the seat. Her eyes are wide, and her fingers are clasping the headrest so hard that her knuckles are white.

I reach in my pocket and pull out my phone. I don't care what they say. If he hits us again I'm calling 9-1-1.

The truck follows us for a couple of miles, but when we turn onto the road to the lake he keeps going. I lay my phone down and fall back onto the seat.

"Bye-bye, asshole." Chloe waves at him.

Paige takes one hand off the wheel and punches Chloe in the arm.

"What the fuck?" Chloe says.

"That guy's psycho and you're antagonizing him!"

"I ain't afraid of that old fart," Chloe says.

She's lying. I saw how scared she looked.

The joint's gone now, so I roll down my window and breathe in the fresh woodsy air. I love this place. Dad used to bring me here sometimes after him and Mom got divorced. He has a new family now.

Paige drives until it looks like we're coming out the other side of the park.

"I thought we were going to the lake," I say.

"We're not going into the *actual* park." Paige rolls her eyes at me. I sit back and shut up.

"There's a place a further down that nobody knows about," Chloe says. "It's more private."

"Minutes later, we come to a gravel road with a rope tied across the entrance. Paige gets out and unties the rope. We drive though.

"Aren't you going to tie the rope back?" Chloe asks.

"Nah," Paige says.

We drive a little further, and the road turns to pavement again.

"We come here all the time," Chloe says. "They closed this section a off long time ago. I think some kids got hurt here or something."

"If you call getting brutally raped and murdered getting hurt." Paige flips a cigarette butt out the window.

"Don't listen to her," Chloe tells me. "She's full of shit."

"You're full of shit," Paige says.

We pull into to an overgrown parking lot. Down below, there's an open patch of land with an old metal grill sticking out of the ground and two broken down picnic tables. The whole area is shaded except for over one of the tables.

""I gotta pee," Chloe says as we walk down the little grade to the clearing.

"Why didn't you go at the store?" Paige asks.

"I didn't have to then."

Paige and I grab the stuff while Chloe runs into the woods. At first, I think she's going to squat behind a tree; then I see her go inside a graffiti-covered outhouse. That thing has to be ancient. It's made out of wood and there's a little crescent moon carved into the door.

The trees here are gigantic with twisted roots that look like snakes slithering up from the ground. One of them made a big ugly crack in the parking lot. Another is making one of the picnic tables lopsided. It's as if nature is trying to destroy all the human stuff.

As we walk to the middle of the clearing, I get the feeling that the trees are watching and listening to every word we say. Pot always makes me paranoid.

Paige sits on top of the sunny picnic table and starts rolling another joint. Her fingers just glide right over the paper making it look easy. It's not. I still haven't figured out how I'm going to smoke the rest of the bag. Maybe if I give her a little, she'll roll a couple for me.

"So… where'd you get this weed?" she asks. "It's been pretty dry around here since Jessie got busted."

"From my cousin," I say.

She frowns and lights the joint. "Can you get more?"

Before I can answer, Chloe starts screaming.

We both jump up and run to the outhouse.

Paige flings the door open, and Chloe is sitting on the seat with her shorts around her ankles.

"What the fuck is your problem?" Paige asks her.

"There's a big-ass spider in here." Chloe points up.

A big yellow and black garden spider is looking down at us from its web in the corner.

"Kill it," Chloe says.

Paige slams the door and walks away.

"*Please* Paige," Chloe cries from inside. "You gotta kill it."

"It won't hurt you," Paige yells over her shoulder. "Besides, I can't reach it."

All of a sudden, everything gets darker. I look up and see a bunch of clouds blocking the sun. A cool breeze whips my hair in my face, and I swipe it away.

"Is it supposed to rain?" I ask Paige when we get back to the table. She shrugs and hands me the joint.

Chloe comes back a few minutes later. "Toss me a wine cooler, baby." She's looking at me, so I hurry and get her one. "It's dark as fuck out here," she says.

"Dabney said it's going to rain." Paige makes a face.

"Really, Dabney?" Chloe asks me. "Oh, I hope not."

"My turn." Paige jumps up and heads for the outhouse.

I have to pee too, but she called it first, so I sit back down.

"Why didn't you go when we were at the store?" Chloe yells after her.

Paige gives us the finger and keeps on walking.

Chloe climbs on top of the picnic table and lays spread eagle across it. I sit on the bench seat beside her and look up at the sky. The sun peeks out from behind the clouds and it feels warm on my face. After a minute, the clouds come back together, and the sky turns dark again.

"I just love the woods," Chloe says. "I think I must've been a woods nymph in a previous life."

"Woods nympho is more like it." Paige is tucking her shirt in as she walks back to the table.

"Bite me," Chloe tells her.

"Whatever," Paige says. "Let's go for a walk."

"Wait," I say. "I have to pee too."

I jog over to the outhouse. When I open the door, the smell of shit hits me in the face. I take a deep breath before stepping inside. Somebody left a roll of toilet paper by the hole, so I pull some big pieces off and lay them across the seat. Rumor is, Chloe has crabs, and I'm not taking any chances.

I sit down and look up in the corner. The spider is still in the exact same spot.

I'm almost done when a crack of thunder shakes the little building. I jump off the seat and pull my shorts up without wiping. As I'm fastening them, I hear something scrape against the door of the outhouse. I hear Paige and Chloe giggling.

"What are you guys doing?" The giggling is fainter like they're walking away. I flip the latch on the door and push. Nothing happens.

"Paige? Chloe?" I listen for a minute, but I can't hear them anymore.

I jerk the handle back and forth and throw my weight into the door. It still won't open. "Come on, you guys," I yell. "It really stinks in here."

Thunder rumbles overhead and big raindrops plop, like rotten eggs, on the old tin roof.

"Chloe!" I scream. "*Please*, let me out." My voice sounds weak and pathetic. This can't be happening.

I try to peep through the little moon in the door, but it's up so high that I can't see much. I notice that there are cracks between some of the boards. I peek through one and… *Those bitches!* Paige and Chloe have wedged a tree branch between the ground and the door. What the hell? Did they plan this all along? Is this why they invited me in the first place?

I kick the door hard then cry out as pain shoots up my foot. I forgot that I wore sandals today instead of the old sneakers I usually wear. It feels like I broke my toe.

I fall back onto the edge of the seat and pull my foot up into my lap. It looks okay, but my big toe is throbbing. I wipe my face with the hem of my shirt and look up in the corner. All my yelling must've scared the spider because she's not in her spot anymore. "It's okay," I say. "I'm harmless."

It's raining harder outside. It sounds like someone's flinging pebbles at the roof. It's getting darker too. I try not to cry, but I can feel the tears forming in my eyes. To hell with them! I'm calling Mom.

I change position and feel around in my pockets. My phone! Where the hell is my phone? Then I remember. I left it lying on the back seat of the car. *Shit!* This means that I am at their mercy, and if I know anything for sure about Paige and Chloe it's that they are *not* merciful. I think about the time Paige thought the new girl was scoping out her boyfriend. What was her name again? Oh yeah, Maria. Paige sat in the lunchroom and waited until Maria walked by then kicked her legs out from under her.

I can still see that poor girl lying on the floor with spaghetti on her chest and milk in her hair while the entire lunchroom laughed and pointed. After that, everyone, me included, steered clear of Maria. Why did I do that? What did Maria ever do to me?

I look for a crack on the side of the outhouse facing the parking lot. I find one, but the rain is so dense it's hard to see. I press my face up to the crack. I can see the white outline of Paige's mom's car. Thank God! They're probably just messing with me. They'll let me out in a few minutes. We'll all have a laugh, maybe smoke another joint. Everything will be cool.

I try to see if Paige and Chloe are inside the car, but I can't tell. The rain is really coming down now. I can see little streams of muddy water running down from the parking lot.

I see something else too – something red. Is that? It is! A red pickup truck is parked on the other side of the lot!

Oh my God! Have Paige and Chloe seen it?

I want to call out and warn them, but I'm too scared. I move around inside the outhouse and peek through every crack. I can't see anything else, so I give up and sit back down. I want to cry. I want to scream! But I don't know where the curly-haired man is. What if he's standing right outside the door?

My heart is beating faster than I can count, and I'm starting to hyperventilate. I bend forward, placing my hands over my face and try to calm down. I tell myself that I'm just being silly, and that there's nothing to worry about. Then I remember the look on the curly-haired man's face and how he purposely rammed into our car.

He's going to find me. Any minute now, he's going to burst through that door and grab me, and there's nothing I can do about it. I'm trapped here like a rat in a cage.

I'm worried about Paige and Chloe too. But, if he attacked them, wouldn't I have heard something? I'm pretty sure those two wouldn't go down without a fight. Maybe they left for their walk before he got here. Maybe they're holed up inside an old shed or something. They must be. They have to be!

Who am I kidding? Even if they are okay, he's just gonna wait and grab them as soon as they come back. He's gonna grab them and then he's gonna… Oh God!

And, when he's done with them, he's gonna come looking for me! He knows there are three of us. He looked right at me. Oh, why am I so fucking stupid? I should never have come here. Those girls don't really like me. They just wanted my pot.

I'm starting to freak out again, so I force myself to stop thinking about it. Instead, I think about Maria and how scared and embarrassed she looked when Paige tripped her. If I live through this, I'm gonna march straight up to Maria and tell her I'm sorry. If I live…

How long have I been here? It seems like hours, but I'm sure it's not that long. I can almost feel the stench of other people's shit clinging to my skin. My eyes are stinging, my toe hurts, and I'm thirstier than I've ever been. But mostly, I'm sleepy - *so* sleepy. Mixing Dramamine, alcohol, and pot probably wasn't a good idea.

The rain is tapering off now, and the thunder sounds far away. I should probably look through the crack to see if the truck's still out there, but I'm too scared. If I see that stupid thing again, I'm pretty sure that I'll pass out from fright.

The rain must've caused the temperature to drop because it's starting to get chilly. I tuck my legs up under my chin and stretch my t-shirt over them. It throws me off balance a little, but I don't want to lean against that wall. It's dirty and gross and covered with spider webs.

My head starts to nod, and I don't care anymore. Can't stay… awake.

I'm standing in the woods. The rain has gone, and sunlight is trickling down through the trees. I see a clearing up ahead with a long serving line like the one in our school cafeteria at lunchtime. Wait! That *is* the cafeteria line! I recognize some of the kids, and there's Mrs. Rooney, in her white hairnet, is scooping something onto their trays. They're far away, but I can hear a soft mushy sound every time she ladles out another scoop.

Someone's giggling. I turn to see Maria standing behind me. She's wearing a pretty pink blouse, but it's stained with spaghetti sauce and drops of milk are running down her face and neck.

"I'm sorry for what they did to you." I say. "And, I'm sorry for pretending like you didn't exist."

Maria smiles at me, and I know that we're going to be friends.

There's a crash like thunder and everything looks a little darker. I hear a loud shriek in the distance. I turn my head, and there it is again- a terrifying sound.

"That's Chloe!" I say. "We have to help her!" I look around, but Maria is gone.

I don't know what else to do, so I start running toward the sound. As I zigzag through the trees, I notice that some of them have faces embedded in their trunks. I keep running, trying not to look at them. The next thing I know, I'm standing in front of the outhouse.

The branch is still wedged in front of the door, and loud screams are coming from inside. I hurry over and yank on the branch, but it's wedged in tight. "Hold on Chloe!" I yell.

She must've heard me because the screaming has stopped.

I look around for something to use for leverage. I search for what seems like forever, but all I can find are piles of spaghetti and puddles of milk. Finally, I see a fallen tree. I pry one of the limbs off and run back to the outhouse.

I place my limb crossways under the branch and pull. The limb breaks in two. "Damn it! You okay in there, Chloe?"

She doesn't answer me.

Grabbing the branch with both hands, I dig my feet in and pull as hard as I can. The branch gives way, and I fall on my ass into a puddle of milk.

I scramble to my feet and open the door. "Chloe?"

She's in there, but she's not moving, and she's leaning across the seat at a weird angle. I step inside and stare down in horror.

Head tilted back and eyes wide open, Chloe is covered with thousands of thin silvery threads. The garden spider is peeping out from inside her gaping mouth watching her babies scamper back and forth across their new playground.

I throw my head back and scream. The movement knocks me off the seat, and I land on my ass on the outhouse floor.

"Hey!" a man's voice says. "Is somebody in there? Hang on. I'll get you out."

I hear lot of scuffing, then strong arms are lifting me up and out.

"I could use some help over here!" The voice yells by my ear.

The arms are still holding me as the nice man lays me back across his lap. I look up at the red and blue lights flashing through the trees as a dozen strangers crowd around, all of them staring down at me.

"Looks like this one got lucky," somebody says. "I wonder why he locked her in the outhouse like that?"

"Who knows," someone else says. "Maybe he was saving her for last. Too bad about those other two."

Yvonne T. Tibbs

CHAPTER 14

"They sure cuss a lot," Numo said.

"That's teenagers for you," Peg said. "They think it makes them look... tougher, I guess."

"Do you cuss?" Numo asked.

"Sometimes," Peg admitted. *Especially lately.*

While reading to the beast-child sitting on the floor by her feet, Peg had paid little attention to the words, as her mind was busy plotting escape. If she could win Numo's trust, she might just have a chance.

Placing the book on the bed, she attempted to reach out and pat the boy's head. But, just before it met with his pale cadaverous skin, her hand drew back, as if of its own volition. Fortunately, Numo didn't seem to notice.

"Well, I don't know about you," Peg said, attempting to sound cheery, "but, I'm starving. What say, we raid the kitchen?"

Numo gave her a sidelong look. "Promise you won't try to escape?"

"Cross my heart." She traced an invisible X across her chest.

"All right. But, you better not be lying."

When they reached the door, Numo simply placed his hand in front of a small, barely visible pad on the wall to the right of the doorframe. He walked out, but Peg hesitated. Was that the sound of Macushla's legs slithering down the hall?

"Where's your mother?" Peg whispered, clinging to the doorjamb.

"She's visiting the lab. She practically lives there."

The lab? Peg didn't like the sound of that. As they proceeded down a white, unadorned corridor, she fought the urge to bolt somewhere, anywhere away from the freakish little fiend at her side. But, he was the lesser of two evils, she reminded herself. Best to stay on his good side until she could find an exit.

"So," she began, keeping her voice low. "Do you have any brothers and sisters, Numo?"

"Hundreds," he replied without looking up. "But, I'm the only one from the first group who survived." He stopped beside a wide glass door, held his palm to the right of it, and stepped inside. "Would you like to see the second group?"

Peeking in from the doorway, Peg observed row upon row of clear, oval shaped vats mounted atop some sort of control panels. They appeared to contain a gray watery substance, and as Peg peered into the one nearest the door, she imagined she could see a small form floating inside it. All at once, a tiny hand with far too many fingers shot up jerkily accompanied by a sloshing sound.

"Come on in," Numo said. "Don't you want to see?"

"N... not right now," Peg said.

Numo shrugged and rejoined her in the hallway. The next door opened to a small kitchenette similar to that of the hospital break room. She opened the refrigerator and stood staring into it, unable to make sense of what she was seeing. Piled high atop metal trays were dozens of what looked like Mac's famous loose-meat sandwiches. "Wh-where did you get these?"

"You don't want those," Numo said. He pointed to a cabinet mounted out of his reach on the wall. "I think there are some cookies in there."

But, Peg was picturing Mac's face when he handed her one of the sandwiches. For a moment, she had thought he looked… what? Nervous? Expectant? Turned on? She shuddered and wrapped her arms about herself.

"Peg?"

"What? Oh, sorry." Pushing the thought form her mind, Peg retrieved a box of wafers and choked down as many as she could while trying to think of a way to get near the front entrance again. "Numo," she began, "Do you remember that big scary guy that tried to hypnotize me?"

"Who? Dimitri?"

"I didn't catch his name."

"Yes. What about him?"

"Has he ever hypnotized you before?"

The boy made a disgusted sound. "Dimitri has no power over me."

This was the response Peg was hoping for. "So… what? You just ignore him?"

"You could say that. It's a question of will."

"And, your mind is stronger than his?" Peg shot him a look she hoped was skeptical.

"You don't believe me?"

Peg steeled herself as Numo's big goggling eyes swept over her. Could he read her mind? She attempted to clear her thoughts just in case.

"Follow me," he said at last.

Numo led her back into the hallway and around the corner to an elevator. When they stepped inside, Peg saw that they were currently on the second floor. The buttons on the keypad were labeled 1-3 as well as a capitol B at the bottom, which she assumed stood for basement. If Numo took her back to the first floor, where she had encountered the monster, she could try and bust out of this nightmarish place through the same door by which she had entered.

Oh, please, press 1.

But, Numo pressed B, and the flame of hope burning in Peg's chest flickered and grew smaller. Why were they going to the basement?

The elevator descended for what seemed like an unusually long time. When at last the doors opened, they were facing another long corridor. Unlike the plain white walls in the upstairs hallway, however, these were unlit and appeared to be... *moving.*

As she stared into the dark, cavernous tunnel, a long forgotten image pushed its way to the front of Peg's mind, and she was transported back to June 2, 1991. Sad-eyed and boney, it was Peggy Sue Starling's 8th birthday party. Well, it was supposed to be. Daddy had been gone for over a year by then, her best friend Samantha was sick, and her mother was stuck at work in the local nursing home.

That left only Grandpa, deaf as a fence post, and Peggy's two older brothers, Jack and Dwayne. Pretending to feel sorry for her, the boys asked if she'd like to go spelunking with them. Ever the tomboy, Peggy readily agreed.

The boys took her to a cave set deep in the hills, coaxed her inside, and left her there. Her brothers later claimed that they'd done it as a prank, intending to go back for her in due time. But, boys being boys, they had found other mischief to get into and it was Uncle Tim who found her, chilled to the bone and terrified some six hours later.

"What are you waiting for?" Numo's melodious voice was tainted with impatience.

Peg jumped then, not wishing to anger the boy, she grit her teeth and stepped out of the elevator. The air felt even colder than it had upstairs, triggering an outbreak of goosebumps across her arms and legs. As the elevator doors slid shut behind them, Peg tried not to scream as she imagined being sealed forever inside a deep, inescapable tomb.

Again, spotting movement in the wall beside her, she sprang back, nearly bowling Numo over.

"Hey! Watch it!" he exclaimed.

"Sorry. Did you see that?"

"What, the fish?"

Did he say fish? It was then, Peg realized that the walls and ceiling were made entirely of glass, behind which, the watery world she'd seen in the grand foyer extended upward and outward. Far above, faint ribbons of light seemed to float along the outer edges of the thalassic realm, but directly overhead a dense unmoving mass cast everything beneath it in shadow.

"We're under the house," Numo said, as if privy to her thoughts. He flipped an invisible switch illuminating dozens of submerged spotlights pointing out into the water. "Wait here," he said, "I'll go find Dimitri."

As soon as the boy disappeared from view, Peg turned her attention back to the elevator. Her heart sank when she saw that the only means of accessing it was another blank pad beside the door.

All at once, she felt an alarming sensation deep inside her brain. She wasn't sure how she knew, yet she felt certain that someone, somewhere was summoning her. She quailed as she recalled Macushla's enigmatic contact and how it had so easily rendered her weak and malleable. But, this seemed different. Peg sensed that this communication, psychic or whatever the hell it was, was nonthreatening in nature. It was obviously not coming from the elevator, so she turned and walked in the only direction she could.

As she proceeded through the remarkable passageway, Peg felt as if she was walking across the bottom of the ocean. Just a few feet away, the water was alive with color. Unfamiliar plant life vivid in shades of pink, orange, and green reached their searching fingers ever upward while gently swaying to an inaudible beat. It must be some kind of coral reef Peg decided, although she'd never actually seen one.

There were also all manner of fish and things she'd only seen on television or during her one and only trip to The Newport Aquarium. Among them were something that resembled a giant crawdad, breathtakingly beautiful jellyfish, tiny seahorses, and a skinny little critter with a long pointed snout. A school of curious blue and yellow fish swam alongside her while a large manta ray drifted slowly overhead. As fear was replaced by fascination, Peg almost forgot what she was searching for. Then there it was again, a subconscious message, urgent and pleading.

Without warning, all the sea life that had been trailing along beside her scattered and disappeared. What had scared them all away? Was it the monster called Dimitri? Drawing to a stop, Peg tried to decide what to do. Should she run back to the elevator? Scream for Numo to come to her aid?

It was too late. Slithering out of the depths, his long, glistening body undulating behind his big ugly head, Dimitri gazed at her from behind the glass. As the lighted protrusion beneath his chin began to wriggle back and forth, Peg felt as if gravity had given up its hold on her and she was floating slowly and deliberately into a warm protective cocoon. A soft iridescent light appeared suffusing everything except for a small, rectangular shaped object drifting toward her. It was the book! As Peg watched, the cover fell open and a voice, deep and masculine, began to read.

Yvonne T. Tibbs

CHAPTER 15
The Penance

"Daddy! Daddy! Daddy!"

I adore Grace. From the moment they handed me that red-faced little bundle in the delivery room, I was smitten. On this particular day, however, the sound of that two-syllable word spilling over my daughter's tongue made me cringe. I saved the document I was working on and turned toward the open screen door. "What is it, Grace? What's the matter now?"

She came to me cheeks flushed and eyes, her mother's eyes, flowing with tears, and I felt another rift in my heart. "He killed her!" Grace's youthful voice was thick with emotion. "Echo killed my little mermaid!"

Echo was the Chocolate Labradoodle Courtney and I bought Grace last year on her fifth birthday. Like Grace, the house, and the hefty credit card bills, the dog was yet another responsibility I was to bear alone – since Courtney, left us.

Looking down at my daughter, I noticed that her hands and knees were caked with mud and something else - something *red*. Alarmed, I placed my hands beneath her armpits and lifted her aloft. "What's all over you, honey? Is that … blood?" I turned her this way and that, searching for the wound.

"I told you," Grace sobbed, her slender body tensing in my grasp. "It's from my mermaid. Echo *killed* her."

I reached over to close my laptop. The constant interruptions were making it all but impossible to get any further with my novel. But, with all those bills hanging over my head, I couldn't afford a sitter.

"Okay, Grace. Let's go outside, and you can show Daddy what happened." I got up, stretched the kinks from my back, and took her small, damp hand into mine.

Our cottage sits less than fifty feet from the skinny, ever-winding St. Joseph River. If my wife were still alive, she'd have given me ten kinds of hell for allowing Grace to play outside unsupervised. But, Grace knew her boundaries. I'd drilled them into that sweet little head of hers since she was three.

Spotting us, Echo rushed up, barking and circling our legs.

"Bad, dog!" Grace scolded. "Bad, Echo!"

Echo lowered his tail and cowered. Angry words from his master were worse than a blow. But, a dog's shame is fleeting, and seconds later, he was back at our heels again.

Grace led me to a long, thin strand running parallel to the river inside which water collected when the river was up. *I have got to hire a babysitter.* I told myself. I'd been such a fool, thinking a six-year-old could maintain boundaries.

"You were playing here?" I asked. "You know this is out of bounds, Grace You're not to set foot past the picnic table."

"I'm sorry, Daddy." She lowered her head.

"So this is where…?"

"This is where I found Gloria," Grace sputtered, "my mermaid." And, the tears started afresh.

Scooping her up, I kissed her cheek then turned and yelled at the dog until he ran back to the house.

Lowering Grace to the ground, I walked over to examine the rivulet more closely. I'd assumed she was referring to one of her Barbie dolls. Echo loved to gnaw on them, and it was nothing to find a detached leg here or mangled head there. But, that would not have explained the blood.

"Okay, Grace," I said. "Where exactly was this mermaid?"

Overcome with emotion, she could only point.

I followed her shaking finger to the other end of the strand. At first, I saw nothing but muddy water and paw prints; then I noticed several splotches of darkened blood. I walked to the other side and got down on my haunches for a better look. It was definitely blood, and floating atop, what looked like, short strands of silvery hair was a pale cylindrical object.

I dropped to my knees placing both hands on the ground and leaned closer. A little over an inch long, it resembled a bent twig, but the color was all wrong. Gathering the object into my palm, I let the dark bloody water drain out through my fingers. As I stood, pulling the object up to my face, I very nearly dropped it again.

There in my hand, was a tiny severed arm.

For a moment, I couldn't speak. When I recovered my voice, it sounded hoarse and weak. "So this belonged to… "

"Gloria." Grace peered up at me with tear stained cheeks.

Holding my discovery out away from my body, I pulled her up onto my hip with my free hand. "I'm sorry about your mermaid,' I said. "Let's go back inside and get you cleaned up. Okay?"

Though still in mourning, Grace rewarded me with a bright toothy smile, so eager was she for a few minutes of my attention.

After taking her bath and nibbling some leftover pizza I nuked in the microwave, Grace drifted off to sleep. Despite his heinous crimes, all was forgiven, and Echo was, as usual, curled up by her side.

I had placed the arm in a shallow saucer on the counter in the kitchen. The instant Grace fell asleep I hastened back for another look. Sitting in the shadows at the foot of Grace's bed, I had managed to convince myself that I was mistaken. The arm wasn't flesh and bone, just a remarkable facsimile. It's amazing what they were doing with children's toys nowadays. But beneath the 75-watt bulb in the overhead light, I could see that more blood had eked onto the plate. There was also a barely visible piece of white bone poking out the top of the arm where, if not for Echo, a shoulder would be.

I jerked open the "junk drawer" beside the sink and rummaged about. I then darted to the living room where I ransacked my father's old roll top desk. Finally, I found what I was looking for – a magnifying glass. I grabbed my desk lamp and returned to the kitchen.

After drying my sweaty palms, I placed the plate beneath the lamp. Holding my breath, I peered through the eyeglass. There was no longer any doubt. Through the lens, I discerned the irregular shades, narrow ridges, and near-invisible hairs indicative of human, or *humanoid*, skin. It really was an arm. But not, *obviously*, an ordinary arm. In addition to the size, the appendage had a greenish hue, and between the four fingers of its hand (no thumb) was a thin, fibrous webbing.

But, what was I to do with it? I noticed that the skin was beginning to look desiccated. If this creature really did come from the river, perhaps it needed to be kept moist. Pulling the corner off a paper-towel, I ran it beneath the faucet, placed it in a different saucer, and carefully laid my specimen on top. I then pushed the new saucer to the back of the countertop, well out of reach of a certain canine.

I returned to the living room, which also served as my office, and restarted the laptop. I googled tiny mermaids, but all I could find were poorly devised hoaxes and everything you ever wanted to know about Walt Disney's, Ariel. Nevertheless, I continued to search, reading everything on the subject I could find. Surely, if these creatures were real, someone somewhere had captured, or at the very least, seen one.

Sometime after 3:00 AM, I shuffled back into the kitchen to make more coffee. When I glanced at the saucer, I was dismayed to see the arm was gone. I snatched up the paper towel without thinking. The towel was dry, the moisture having evaporated, and a fine dust blew into the air and up my nose making me sneeze.

Cursing my own stupidity, I grabbed a flashlight and went outside where I scoured the riverbank. Finding nothing, I told myself where there was one, there had to be more. With that in mind, I proceeded to the garage where I gathered up my father's fishnets and other paraphernalia and set to work making a trap.

Sometime after sunup, I heard Grace calling me. I hastened back to the house, helped her into her play clothes from the day before, and gave her a bowl of dry cereal.

"What'cha doin out there, Daddy," she asked, as I headed back outside.

"Daddy's doing some very important research," I told her. "You and Echo need to be extra good today so that Daddy can get done with his work. Okay?"

She nodded, her expression resigned. If only I could go back to that moment. I'd pull her into my arms and smother her with kisses.

For the next two days, I was a man obsessed. I refused to leave the river for more than a few minutes at a time, surviving on coffee and stale pretzels while Grace ate peanut butter from a spoon and God only knows what else.

On the afternoon of the third day, I was rewarded for my efforts. Inside my homemade trap, a tiny fish-like creature struggled for freedom.

I was elated! This time, I wasn't going to fuck it up. I'd already dumped Grace's goldfish collection into the river, telling her they'd gone to fish heaven, and filled the tank with rocks, river water, and various other items I thought my special guest might require.

Grace was fascinated too, of course, firing questions at me one after the other while attempting to get a better look at my specimen. I'm afraid I was unkind, telling her to take her stupid barking dog outside and leave me alone.

I spent the next several hours just staring into the tank. In my whole life, I'd never seen a creature so fair with long flowing locks, slender arms, and skin that seemed to glisten with a light of its own. From the waist up, she resembled a woman, or judging from the size of her breasts, an adolescent girl. Just below her navel, however, all humanoid characteristics disappeared. Tiny glistening scales narrowed to a V in front, crept over her buttocks in back, and traveled downward to the end of her serpentine tail. The tail itself was long and thin, no bigger around than a drinking straw. Though I did not do so, if one stretched her out, lengthwise, she probably would've resembled an eel or snake more than a fish.

Other distinctively "aquatic" features were the pointed gills where her ears should be and, just like the arm from the puddle, thin fibrous webbing between each of her dainty fingers with no opposable thumbs. Using the magnifying glass, I also discovered that in lieu of a nose, two teardrop shaped openings centered her tiny oval face.

As for coloring, her eyes were a remarkable shade of green, but the rest is somewhat difficult to describe. Her hair, darker than her body, was the only constant. The rest of her body was a mixture of blues, greens, and silver and that seemed to fluctuate with her movements, or perhaps, with her mood.

Oh, what a fantastic little miracle! But, where did she come from? Was she intelligent? Could she communicate with me? If she could, she had no desire to do so. If not for the mirrored wall behind the aquarium, I couldn't have seen her at all. Hiding behind a cluster of rocks, the timid being curled into herself, clinging to the rocks as if for dear life.

Of course, my daughter wasn't the only one overcome with curiosity. *What*, I thought, *would happen if I put my finger inside the tank?*

I pulled up my sleeve and dunked my hand into the water. Murmuring what I thought were reassuring words I, ever so slowly, lowered my pointer finger toward her.

She responded by remaining perfectly still, her brilliant eyes glued to the finger. When I was just inches away, I discovered another inhuman characteristic. With lightening fast reflexes, the girl-beast wrapped her hands round my finger, pulled it closer, then opening her jaws abnormally wide, dug long, razor-sharp fangs into my flesh.

With a cry of pain, I jerked my hand out of the aquarium splashing water everywhere.

"Daddy! What happened?"

I looked up to see Grace standing one foot in and one foot out of the screen door. Between her legs, Echo emitted an excited "Yip!"

"I told you to stay outside!" I shouted, the pain in my finger intensifying my reaction.

She blinked and her mouth flew open, shock and dejection unmistakable on her face. The door slammed, and she was gone.

It will be okay, I told myself as I ran my bloody hand beneath the kitchen faucet. I didn't know exactly how yet, but, because of my discovery, we were going to be wealthy beyond our wildest dreams. Soon, I'd be able to buy Grace anything her little heart desired – anything, except perhaps, a mother.

As I lathered dish soap over the surprisingly deep laceration, I imagined agents knocking down my door, eager for a chance to represent me and my book - my *new* book, *The Real Little Mermaid*.

After bandaging my finger, I got my digital camera and took hundreds of snapshots. Pulling myself away, I returned to the laptop and started the painfully slow process of uploading pictures. The first thing I was going to buy with my newfound riches was a state of the art computer, so I could throw this outdated piece of shit in the river.

But, whom should I contact first? Googling marine biologists, I began researching their backgrounds, trying to determine who would be the lucky man or woman to share in my discovery. After a time, I decided on a professor from Maine named Whitman who, in addition to writing several books, had discovered numerous new forms of aquatic life at the bottom of the Atlantic Ocean. I was pretty sure, however, that he hadn't discovered a species quite like mine. Not only that, I'd found my little prize in a relatively shallow river in my own backyard!

And, why *was* she in clear water? One would think an unprecedented species such as this would inhabit an as-yet unexplored part of the ocean? *Oh well,* I thought. *That's what I need the biologist for.* But, I would *not* just be the one who found her. I was going to be her owner, her manager, her…

The pain in my finger had advanced to a growing throb. I looked down to see that the bandage was completely saturated with blood. Damn! I was going to have to wrap it again. On my way to the bathroom, my gaze drifted past the window, and I noticed that the sky outside had darkened considerably.

Grace!

What had I done? A glance at the clock told me it was nearly 9:00 PM. How long ago did I send my six-year-old daughter outside to play? How long had it been since she'd eaten, went to the bathroom, had a *fucking* drink of water? Forgetting my wound, I raced outside, calling for Grace as I went.

She wasn't in the yard, so, following my instincts, I proceeded to the river. I was several yards away when I spotted a dark figure sprawled across the sandy strand. I broke into a run, nearly landing on top of the body before I could stop myself.

It was Echo. In my haste, I'd neglected to grab a flashlight, but the moon was shining bright enough for me to see the blood oozing from the dog's muzzle, legs, and torso.

"Grace!" I threw back my head and screamed my daughter's name into the night. My cries rang hollow, the only response being a chorus of empathetic howls from a neighboring kennel down the road. I ran back to the house and dialed 9-1-1.

Three police cars, a fire truck, and an ambulance arrived within minutes. I guess, due to my panicked blubbering, the dispatch operator wasn't sure what they might find.

First came the interrogation. "When did you last see your daughter? Why was she left outside unattended? Where is the child's mother?" While asking these questions, they watched me with wary expressions and disbelieving eyes. But, I had my own concerns.

What in God's name had killed Echo? Surely, those minute river beings, though vicious, (as evidenced by the persistent throbbing in my finger) couldn't kill a full-grown dog. It would have take dozens, maybe *hundreds* of them. The thought of it filled me with despair. And, what had these demonic little bastards done with my Grace?

I told the police everything, even showed them my little captive inside the fish tank. I remember at one point, growing outraged at their astonished outbursts and in-depth scrutiny of the creature. "Can we just focus on finding my daughter, *please?*" I shouted. Like I had a right to be angry. I had failed her, the only person in the world who loved me, who needed me. I'd tossed her aside in my quest for fame and fortune, and now I might never see my sweet little girl again.

I must've been a wreck because, rather than leave me alone, a young male officer was assigned to watch over me while the authorities began their search. Tall, lanky, with a habit of clearing his throat before speaking, Officer Langley couldn't have been much more than twenty. By that time, I was draped across the living room sofa, physically and emotionally spent.

"You feeling okay, Mr. Ramsey?" Langley asked, taking a seat opposite me. "You don't look so good."

"I haven't slept," I said.

"For how long?"

"I dunno, two… three days."

The medics had re-bandaged the wound on my finger, but I could already see a dark stain spreading through the gauze. It hurt like hell! At some point, I either fell asleep or passed out.

I dreamt I was alone in the house, and someone was knocking at my front door. Pulling myself up from the couch, I stumbled across the room. I was reaching for the doorknob when I noticed the dark fish-smelling water seeping under the door. *What the hell?*

I took a step back and peered out the living room window. It looked as if the entire house was underwater! The river must've flooded. So, who could be knocking at my door?

The frightful sound continued. Slow and deliberate, it seemed as if the door might burst inward with each resounding knock. "Return my daughter to me!" A booming male voice demanded.

"Your d…daughter?" I sputtered. My eyes fell on the aquarium, and I knew of whom he was speaking. "Okay!" I shouted through the door. "Okay! You can have her!"

As I turned back inside, the beige carpet on the living room floor seemed to stretch out beneath me. I could see the aquarium in the distance, but the faster I ran, the further away it became. Suddenly, it was right in front of me, and I saw the mermaid, her tiny hands pressed against the glass. But, something about her looked different. Bending down, my jaw dropped as recognition slapped me in the face. With her slender tail swishing back and forth, holding her body aloft in the water, my daughter Grace peered out at me.

I awoke to the sound of my toilet flushing down the hall. Apparently, Officer Langley had opted to use the facilities. I jerked bolt upright. I had to take her back! If I ever wanted to see Grace again, I had to return the mermaid to the river. And, I had to do it now!

Bounding up from the couch, I ran across the room, grabbed the fish tank, and attempted to lift it. It was only a ten-gallon aquarium, but filled with water, it was no easy feat. Titling it to one side, I poured part of the water directly onto the floor. With adrenaline pulsing through my veins, I hoisted it up, burst through the door, and lumbered toward the river.

Up ahead, I saw beams from individual flashlights as well as one large spotlight and some type of all-terrain vehicle beside the river where I'd found Echo's body. I veered to the right, so as not to encounter them. That meant I'd have to carry my heavy burden twice as far, but I didn't want anyone trying to stop me.

I was nearing the end of the yard when I heard Officer Langley's voice behind me.

"Mr. Ramsey? I need you to come back here, please."

Gathering a strength I never knew I possessed, I quickened my pace. Due to the sound of my own jagged breath and pounding heart, I couldn't hear Langley approaching, but I could *feel* him bearing down on me. Just before reaching the bank, I came upon a large clump of weeds. When I attempted to skirt around it, my foot landed in a patch of sand and began to slide. Losing my grip on the aquarium, I fell belly first onto the bank, knocking the breath from my lungs. With a slapping noise, the mermaid thrashed about on the sand in front of me, the aquarium having landed on its side.

"Mr. Ramsey!" Despite his young age, Officer Langley's voice had acquired an authoritative tone that, under different circumstances, I would not have ignored.

Scrambling to my feet, I scooped the mermaid up and tossed her into the river just as Langley tackled me to the ground.

Weeks passed with no sign of my daughter. The authorities now suspect me, but I don't care what they or anyone else thinks. If they want to put me in prison, so be it. It's no less than I deserve.

A few people are still on my side, however. And, some die-hards are still out there searching. I always force a smile and thank them, but I know they'll never find her. I also know with unfailing certainty that my beloved daughter still lives.

Every day since she left, I have wandered beside the river engaging in one-sided conversations with Grace, the little mermaid, and the mysterious male voice from my dream. Last Tuesday, September 6, was my thirty-first birthday. In my grief-stricken state, I was unaware of the date, much less the fact that it was my birthday. That morning, when I shuffled down the riverbank, I spotted something wedged inside the strand. I ran over and snatched it up only to discover that it was a common, albeit beautifully colored, seashell. It struck me as odd, however. How the devil did a seashell end up in the St. Joseph River?

Running my fingers across its rugged surface, I noticed something unusual on the smooth, pink inside. Now, I possess a treasure more valuable to me than all the fame and riches this miserable world holds. Always in my pocket, within easy reach, is a lovely little cockleshell with words etched inside. It reads simply thus, Happy Birthday Daddy! Love, Grace.

CHAPTER 16

Peg felt a solitary tear slide down her cheek. In front of her the book closed, and she was once again, face to face with the monster Dimitri. It was then, she realized that his swarthy, leather-like skin matched the cover of the book. It was almost as if Dimitri was the book, or the book was Dimitri. And, despite his frightful appearance, still in her warm comforting cocoon, Peg was no longer afraid.

"It was a test," he said, in the same voice that had read to her. As he spoke, Peg noticed that the creature's large, malformed mouth had not moved. "We had to see if you could be trusted to do the right thing."

"I don't understand." To Peg's surprise, she found that she could hear her own thoughts as well. "Are you talking about the book?"

"Yes… the book."

"But how can a book of stories determine anything?"

"It was your reaction we sought."

"We?"

"My brethren and I. Despite being shocked, and at times disgusted, you showed compassion, empathy, and understanding. These qualities, we've learned, are sometimes lacking in most humans."

In spite of the circumstances and the extraordinary truths the words implied, Peg felt nothing but calm and a bit curious. "Well then," she ventured. "How can I help you."

"He is coming." Dimitri's voice had changed, carrying with it a sinister note.

"Who?" The protective cocoon that shrouded Peg was beginning to unravel.

"He," Dimitri answered. "Father to us all. Macushla has disobeyed him and now his wrath is upon us. This place, this *abomination*, is to be destroyed and she, I, and every living thing in it will be returned to the sea where we belong."

"Well, I guess that's a good thing. But, what do you want with me?"

"The boy."

"You… you mean Numo."

"Although himself a mockery of nature, he is but an innocent. Macushla with aid from her human servants have taken the best of us and mixed it with the seed of your race in an effort to reclaim the land and run mankind asunder. Her hatred of humans and their cruel, insensitive treatment of this, our Earth, has made her mad with a desire for revenge. It is too soon, however. It is not yet our time."

"But, what has Numo to do with all this?"

"He is flesh of my flesh. Made from my genes and that of the human they called Rosa. Although half mine, he is also, unfortunately, half human. He will not survive where Father is taking us. It is also my hope that someday, if the child is accepted into your world, he can make a difference, and those living above will welcome those of us from below.

Peg wondered how Dimitri could know these things. Yet, she had no doubt that what he intimated was true.

"You must leave here." His voice was starting to fade. "Take the boy and go. *Now!*"

Peg shuddered as the cocoon ruptured and fell away. She placed both hands on the glass and peered into the water. Dimitri was gone.

"I can't find him anywhere."

Startled, Peg looked down to see that Numo had returned.

"We have to get out of here," she said. Taking the boy's clammy little hand into hers, she started running, half leading, half dragging him behind her.

"What are you talking about?" Numo cried, digging in his heels. "We can't just *leave.*"

"We have to." Peg gasped. "I spoke to Dimitri. He says we're in danger." Reaching the elevator, Peg wrenched the boy's hand up and placed it over the pad beside the doors.

"Ouch!" he squealed. "You're hurting me!"

The doors slid open and Peg leapt inside, dragging Numo with her. "I'm sorry, Numo, but we have to get out of this house."

"Why?"

"It's too much to explain right now. You're going to have to trust me."

"Mother said humans can't be trusted."

"Well you're half human. Can you be trusted?"

When the doors opened, instead of getting out, Peg placed her hands atop the boy's shoulders, staring deep into his brilliant eyes. "Please, Numo. You asked me to be your friend, but the only way we can truly be friends is if we trust each other. I promise, I will answer all your questions once we're safe, but, for now, I really need you to do as I say. Okay?"

Numo stared at her for a moment then slowly nodded his head.

"Good. Let's go!"

"As Peg peeped out into the white hallway lined with doors, Dimitri's words echoed in her mind. *She has taken the best of us and mixed it with the seed of your kind.* What sort of atrocities lurked behind all those doors? She was glad she'd never know. The hallway looked clear, so she motioned for Numo to stay quiet. Treading softly, they walked out of the elevator.

They were halfway down the hall when Peg heard a door opening behind them. She looked back, and her heart nearly stopped. Macushla had emerged from one of the rooms followed by… Was that Dr. Carlson?

As Macushla's hatred washed over her, as palpable as a hand on her throat, Peg's legs grew weak and her resolve began to crumble.

"Run," a disembodied voice commanded.

Turning away, Peg felt the strength returning to her legs. She scooped Numo up in her arms and fled.

"Stop them!" Macushla's voice rumbled like thunder down the hallway, hurting Peg's ears and causing her to stumble. Catching herself, she clutched Numo to her chest and kept going, her legs pumping like pistons beneath her.

At the end of the hall, she skidded nearly slamming into the large metal door in front of her. Once again, she grabbed Numo's hand and placed it over the pad in the wall.

"Numo." Macushla's voice, though only slightly less piercing, now held an almost tender quality. "Come to Mother, Numo."

As she darted through the open door, Peg felt the boy's body tense and start to quiver. In her mind, she thought of reassuring words, but lacked the breath to voice them. Racing out from beneath the stairs, she was relieved to see that they were, once again, inside the grand foyer. *Just a little further.*

"I said, '*Stop them!*'" Macushla's voice reverberated around the room, rattling the mirrors and causing the chandeliers to tinkle above their heads.

"Sh…she won't let m... me leave." Numo muttered, his quivering body making him stutter.

From out of nowhere, people began to appear rushing at them with vacuous eyes and wooden features. As they flashed by, Peg realized that she recognized them. They were all people from the party, Ryan, the Good Samaritan, Sasha, and… "Oh my God!"

Coming straight at her, muscles rippling beneath his white t-shirt, was Mac from the diner. Peg skidded to a stop and tried to skirt around him. She thought that she'd made it when a strong tug on her arm sent her reeling backward. She landed with an audible thud on the floor with Numo sprawled on top of her. Pain coursed through her body like an electric current as the air escaped her lungs, but she managed to maintain her grip on the boy.

Beneath them, the floor started shaking violently. One of the gilded mirrors crashed to the floor. *He's coming! Oh God! He's really coming!*

Meanwhile, Mac seemed to have forgotten his mission and was looking around the vast room with a startled expression. Seizing her chance, Peg scrambled to her feet, then with Numo's skinny limbs wrapped around her torso, made for the exit.

Suddenly, a large fissure opened in the floor directly in front of them, water issuing from it like blood from a wound. Holding her breath, Peg vaulted over the crack and dove into the entryway. When they reached the front door, she couldn't find the pad, so she swung Numo around on her hip, tried the doorknob, and prayed. To her surprise, it turned in her hand and the door flew open. Ignoring the screams and sounds of destruction behind them, Peg ran for her life.

Moments later, the earth shook beneath them and was followed by a deafening sound, similar to that of a giant waterfall. Peg turned to see the house sinking, colossal bursts of water, like tidal waves, crashing down on it from all sides.

Hearing an odd sound, like a melodious whimper, she looked down.

"Mother," Numo murmured.

As destruction raged in front of them, something in her subconscious reminded Peg that the child, yes the child, in her arms, was watching the only home he'd ever known collapsing with the woman he knew as Mother trapped inside. Despite his cool, leathery skin and strange, some might say repulsive, appearance, she coddled him tenderly. "Don't worry," she whispered. "She will be okay."

As the words left her mouth, the certainty of them engulfed Peg with an invisible tidal wave, all her own, as a vision formed in her mind – Macushla Whitman, in all her glory, gliding down the stairs.

CHAPTER 17
The Holes

I wish they'd stop yelling. I put my hands over my ears, but I still hear them. I used to cry when they yell. I don't anymore. I just stay real quiet and wait till it's over.

It's hot back here, and the floor stinks from when our monkey, Juno, threw up. Mommy tried to clean it, but now it just smells like rotten bananas and sanitary powder. It might not be so bad if it was cooler in here, but even with the temperature unit running, it's still way too warm. Yesterday, I heard Mommy on her communicator telling somebody that this is the hottest summer ever.

The sun is *super* bright too. It bounces off the other hovercrafts and hurts my eyes. I look down at the little pink stars on my dress instead. I don't really like dresses, but Mommy made me wear this one cause Aunt Eila created it for me. We're going to visit her today. I can't wait!

"You're not listening," Daddy is saying. "You do what you want. But, I do not want *my* daughter going to the gathering!"

"Well, she's my daughter too, Kai. And, I think – "

"I don't give a damn what you think!"

"Well that's nice. As usual, my opinion means nothing." Mommy turns away from Daddy and starts digging through her purse. She always does that when she's upset. I wonder what she'd looking for.

"Don't get started with that shit again," Daddy says.

"All I'm saying is – "

"And, all I'm saying is, I will not have my daughter associating with Pelagios."

"Is that what the problem is?" Mommy says. "There's just the one family and - "

"That's not the point. *Now*, there's one. Later on, there'll be a dozen. I don't want Rin going there anymore, and that's final!"

"Well, we'll see about that."

Daddy descends to the lower level and initiates the halting device. Mommy and I jerk forward in our seats. We're floating under the thoroughfare.

"What did you say?" Daddy asks Mommy.

Mommy ignores him and looks out her window. Why does she ignore people like that? Does she think it will make them go away? Sometimes, I think she wants me and Daddy to just go away and leave her alone.

"So help me, Chael!" Daddy's shouting now. "If you sneak her there behind my back, there's gonna be hell to pay. You hear me?"

Mommy doesn't answer. She just keeps looking out the window like she sees something interesting. I lean over and squint so I can see it too. There's nothing out there but some empty docking stations and a little patch of grass, all brown and wilty. There are white spots in front of my eyes now. I blink and blink until they go away.

"Did you hear me?" Daddy's not yelling now, but he has a scary look on his face. Please, Mommy. For once, *please* just say yes.

I jump when he grabs her and pee myself a little. Daddy's hand is on the back of her neck, and his fingers are digging in.

"Daddy don't!" I yell.

It's real quiet inside the hovercraft now. The only sound is that disgusting noise Juno makes when he smacks his lips together. Is Daddy gonna hit Mommy? Please don't let him hit her again. I wish I could see his other hand.

Daddy doesn't move for a long time. Then he lets go of Mommy's neck. He scoots back to his side and looks at me through the reflector. I squeeze my legs together so that I don't pee myself again.

"It's okay Babe," he says. "Mommy and I were just talking."

His voice is nice and soft again, the way I like it, but I can see little red marks on Mommy's neck. Poor Mommy. Why didn't she just answer the question?

This is all my fault. I told Daddy that I didn't want to go to the gathering anymore cause I was scared of the Pelagio people with their big googley eyes and scaly skin. The real reason is because it's so long and boring. I just said that cause Daddy hates the Pelagios. He says they should go back to the ocean where they belong. Mommy told me that a long time ago her great aunt adopted a little boy that was half Pelagio and half human. I think that's awesome, but we're not supposed to talk about it.

Mommy is crying now. She told Daddy to kiss her ass.

Oh no! Did the system hear me? The mentor says that the system sees and hears *everything*. Can it hear what I'm thinking too? Does it know I told a lie and that I said a bad word in my head?

Daddy puts the hovercraft into sleep mode. "I'm sorry," he tells Mommy. He tries to put his arm around her, but she smacks it away.

Why do they have to fight all the time? It's their fault I peed my panties, but I'm the one who's going to get punished. A whole day without my communicator. Or, if Daddy's really mad, he might spank me like last time. It hurt so bad. Maybe they won't notice. My panties are just a little damp.

It's getting brighter outside. Mommy and Daddy don't notice cause they have their sun shields on. I tell Daddy there's something wrong with the sun. He tells me to be quiet.

He never listens to me when Mommy's crying. It's not fair. When I cry they always say, "Big girls don't cry." Isn't *she* a big girl?

Juno keeps making funny noises and jumping around inside his carrier. He's been acting weird today, like he's scared or something. I wish he'd settle down. If he starts screeching, Daddy will get all mad again.

I take off my seatbelt and peek over the front seat. Mommy and Daddy are bent over whispering to each other. She's letting him touch her now. I bet I have to go back to the stupid gathering after all. Like Mommy said, there's only one Pelagio family that goes there, and they have to sit in the humidity section. I've never talked to them, but the little girl waved at me once.

When I was little, I really was scared of the Pelagios. But, that was before the Pelagio man started visiting me in my dreams. I tried telling Mommy about my dreams - about the rumbling sound and the skinny Pelagio man who visits me and tells me about his big shiny palace under the sea. He says that I'm a very good girl and that some day I can come and live there with him there forever. Mommy just told me to shut up and quit being silly. It makes me so mad. I wish the Pelagio man really would take me away. Then she'd be sorry. Maybe. She probably wouldn't even care.

What was that? It sounded like the rumbling from my dreams. I always hear it just before the Pelagio man comes. But, why would he be coming now? It's not even nighttime.

There it is again! Can't Mommy and Daddy hear it? Oh. It looks like they put their earbuds in. They always wear earbuds. I think it's so they don't have to listen to me.

The rumbling keeps getting louder. I wish it would stop. It scares me. I scream and Juno starts screeching. Mommy and Daddy take out their earbuds and turn around.

"What's wrong?" Mommy says.

"What the hell are you screaming about?" Daddy says.

"The rumbling. Didn't you hear it?"

Daddy listens, but it's stopped now. He leans over the seat. I can't see his eyes cause of the sun shields, but his mouth is frowning. "I don't hear anything."

"Damn it, Rin!" Mommy's talking through her teeth again. "I've had enough of your shit today!"

"Well, there you have it," Daddy says to Mommy. "See what your gathering has done for our daughter? Now, she's telling lies."

"You can't blame *that* on the gathering," Mommy says. "Rin's just trying to get attention. She does it all the time."

Daddy says he's gonna bust my ass if I do it again. He takes the hovercraft out of sleep mode and we're moving again. They never listen to me! I hate them both! I wish they were dead! Then I could get different parents – nicer ones.

No… I don't want them to die. I just want them to disappear like they were never really here.

Juno starts yowling and banging on the inside of his carrier. His squishy toy is on the seat, so I crack open the door of his carrier open and shove it inside. He clicks his tongue and shoves the toy in his mouth.

I cross my arms and scrunch down in my seat. Did I just imagine the rumbling? But, it sounded so real, and I'm pretty sure Juno heard it too. Besides, if you tell somebody something you think is true, that's not lying. Is it? When I grow up, I'm gonna select a little girl. I'm gonna name her Tia and create pretty things for her and never punish her or yell at her. And, when she tells me stuff, *I'm* going to believe her.

Juno spit his toy out, and he's screeching again.

"Can't you do something with him?" Daddy says to Mommy.

"Rin, get Juno's bottle out of my bag," Mommy says.

I crawl in the floor by Mommy's tote bag and look for Juno's bottle. He doesn't really need a bottle, but it helps to keep him quiet. Sometimes, Mommy holds him like a baby and feeds it to him. Meko, the boy who lives in the habitat above ours told me a secret once. He said that my mommy told his mommy that when they did the selection process, she wanted a boy, but Daddy wanted a girl, so they got me instead. I think she likes to pretend that Juno is the baby boy she wanted. I'm pretty sure she likes him better than me.

I see Juno's bottle, so I grab it. The sun shields Grandma created for me are in there too, so I put them on and climb back in my seat. I crack the carrier door open again and show Juno his bottle. "Here," I say. "Want it?"

He stops screeching and reaches for it.

We're almost to Aunt Eila's habitat. There's that big nature globe at the end of their street. I should probably say, Aunt Eila *and* Uncle Grey's habitat. I don't like Uncle Grey. He's always kissing me, and his whiskers scratch my cheek. At least, I'll get to see Rainy. I bet she's already there waiting for me. Rainy lives in the habitat beside Aunt Eila. She's only six and a half, not seven like me, but she's real funny, and she's got curly blonde hair. I wish I had curly blonde hair.

I wonder if the rumbling noise will come back. I keep listening for it, but all I can hear is Juno sucking on his bottle.

We're pulling into Aunt Eila's driveway! Uncle Grey is walking out to the docking station to meet us. He's wearing sun shields too, and he has a stupid look on his face.

I get out of the hovercraft. It's so hot! I can hardly breathe. Uncle Grey picks me up and kisses my cheek.

"Have a little accident, honey?" he whispers to me.

I hate him!

"It's hotter than hell out here," he says to Daddy. "You guys hear the news? There was a giant earthquake in Mexico. Apparently, it tore down the last of the old wall."

"Really?" Mommy says.

"Really," Uncle Grey says. "Come on in. They're showing it on the global monitor."

Mommy pulls Juno out of his carrier and tells Daddy to grab her bag. They walk off and leave me standing in the docking station. I don't care. I'm gonna find Rainy and tell her about the rumbling. Should I tell her about the Pelagio man from my dreams? She might laugh at me.

I look around and see her standing in front of Aunt Eila's habitat. She's smiling, at me, and her hair is all sparkly in the sunlight.

I start walking toward her, but the ground feels all weird and crumbly. I look down and when I look back up Rainy's not there anymore. Where'd she go?

The sun is so bright it's getting hard to see even with my sun shields on. It feels like I'm walking through a bright, white nothing. And, it's *so* hot! My dress is damp, and it's sticking to my skin. At least, Mommy and Daddy won't know I peed my panties now. Unless stupid Uncle Grey tells them.

A drop of sweat goes in my eye, so I take off my sunshields and rub it. I take a couple more steps and I can see something in front of me. It looks like that ugly statue in front of Aunt Eila's place. Rainy was standing beside it when I saw her before. She's gone now, but there's a funny-looking hole in the pavement where she was standing. It's kinda big and all bumpy around the edges like the clouds I draw sometimes. Where did it come from? And, why is everything so quiet?

I think of something and get a funny feeling in my tummy. Did Rainy fall in the hole? I don't want to, but I get down on my knees to look. The pavement burns my knees, so I push the bottom of my dress down under them.

It's dark down in the hole. I squint real hard and try to see the bottom, but I can't. Did Rainy really fall in there? Oh *please* let it not be true, not Rainy! My tears fall in the hole and…

Wait! Something's moving way down at the bottom. It's coming closer!

I hear a crunching noise, like the sound Juno makes when he's eating peanuts, and the hole gets a little bigger. I jump back and fall on my butt. I have to go get Daddy. He'll know what to do.

I stand up and wipe off my dress. Mommy will be so mad if it gets dirty. My eyes are watering bad, so I take off my sun shields and rub them some more. I put my sun shields back on and look around.

I see more holes.

There's bunches of them all around. Most of them are little, but, if I watch one long enough, I can see it getting bigger.

I look where Aunt Nancy's habitat should be, but I can't see that far. Where are all the grownups? Why did they leave Rainy and me out here by ourselves? Didn't they see the holes?

"Daddy!" I yell loud as I can.

I start running, but my foot slips in a puddle of water. Water? Where did that come from? I look back at the big hole Rainy fell in, and there's water coming out of it now. That must've been what I saw when I looked inside it. I start running again, but Mommy made me wear my slick shoes today, and I can't stop sliding. I throw my hands out and - *Wham!*

My sunshields fly off, and my knees hit the pavement. It hurts real bad, and now my dress is wet and dirty. Mommy's going to kill me. But, it's not my fault. There's water everywhere. It's coming from those stupid holes.

I try to look for my sunshields, but the white nothing burns my eyes. I close them and feel around with my fingers. Everything I touch feels hot and wet.

I find my sunshields and put them back on. They're wet too, but at least I can see a little now. I try to stand up, but I hear a big "*crack*" and the ground starts moving. A hole is opening up under my hand. I jerk it back.

I want my daddy! I start to cry, but then I hear something. I stop crying so I can hear it better.

It sounds like Juno! He's screeching like crazy. He sounds far away.

"Daddy!" I yell. My voice sounds dry and scratchy like Grandma's.

"*Daddy!*" The ground moves again, and one of my legs slides into a hole.

I can hear sirens now. They sound like the ones that go off when the system says a tornado is coming.

There's something else too. It's the rumbling sound from my dreams!

"Rin! Rin, where are you?"

It's Daddy!

"Over here!" I yell loud as I can, but with all the sirens and the rumbling noise, I don't know if he can hear me.

I think I see somebody. Is it Daddy? No, it can't be. He's way too skinny.

I'm sliding into the hole! I dig my fingernails into the pavement and try to hold on, but it hurts so much, and I'm still sliding. Is this how the system punishes you when you're bad? Oh please, Mr. System! Please, don't hurt me! I'm sorry for thinking bad things. I don't hate anybody. Not *really*. I promise, I'll always tell the truth, and I'll never think bad stuff again.

Somebody is screaming. Is that Mommy? Somebody else is yelling. Why do they sound so far away?

Somebody grabbed my arm! They're pulling me out!

"Daddy!" I look up, but it's not Daddy. It's the Pelagio man from my dreams! I can't see very good, but I know it's him cause his fingers are cold and damp. They feel so good on my skin. He bends down so I can see his face. It's shiny and smooth, and he has lots of pointy teeth. It's not a mean face though, and I'm pretty sure he's smiling at me. I wrap my arms around his neck.